Alexis's
cupcake
cupid

This book is a work of fiction. Any references to historical events, real people, or real places are used fictitiously. Other names, characters, places, and events are the product of the author's imagination, and any resemblance to actual events or places or persons, living or dead, is entirely coincidental.

SIMON SPOTLIGHT
An imprint of Simon & Schuster Children's Publishing Division
1230 Avenue of the Americas, New York, New York 10020
First Simon Spotlight paperback edition February 2015
Copyright © 2014 by Simon & Schuster, Inc.
All rights reserved, including the right of reproduction
in whole or in part in any form.
SIMON SPOTLIGHT and colophon are registered
trademarks of Simon & Schuster, Inc.
Text by Elizabeth Doyle Carey
Chapter header illustrations and design by Laura Roode
For information about special discounts for bulk purchases, please contact
Simon & Schuster Special Sales
at 1-866-506-1949 or business@simonandschuster.com.
Manufactured in the United States of America 0115 FFG
2 4 6 8 10 9 7 5 3 1
ISBN 978-1-4814-2865-1 (hc)
ISBN 978-1-4814-2864-4 (pbk)
ISBN 978-1-4814-2866-8 (eBook)
Library of Congress Catalog Card Number 2014953952

Alexis's cupcake cupid

by coco simon

Simon Spotlight
New York   London   Toronto   Sydney   New Delhi

CHAPTER 1

Table 4 Two

$\mathcal{P}$ink sparkly sugar?"

Katie peered into her shopping basket. "Check."

"Red food coloring?" I continued.

"Check."

"Heart-shaped Red Hots?"

"Check."

"Red-and-white–striped cupcake wrappers?"

"Check."

"Red gel frosting?"

"Check."

"Yay! Time to check out!" I said cheerfully.

I led the way to the register at Baker's Hollow, the baking supplies store at the mall, and the Cupcake Club's home away from home. We had just been asked by a friend of Emma's mom—somewhat last minute—to bake two dozen cupcakes for a ladies' Valentine's Day luncheon tomorrow. Today is Saturday and the real Valentine's Day is Monday, so we had decided to shop for the supplies together, just for fun. Since I run the finances for our baking club (with the other members' skills as follows: Mia is in charge of style and appearance, Emma is in charge of marketing and publicity, and Katie is in charge of recipes), I had the money and was in charge of paying and then logging the purchase into my newly automated Excel spreadsheet on my tablet. (It replaced my leatherbound accounts ledger, which was running out of pages, anyway.)

The plan today was to get supplies for our Valentine's cupcakes, buy Valentine's Day cards for our families, head back to Emma's to whip up cupcakes, and *then* maybe a sleepover. But first we needed lunch.

In the food court, a new Asian street-food place had just opened, and we had to check it out. Emma loves spicy Asian food, and so does Mia. Katie likes all types of cuisines, and I don't like spicy food at all, but Emma and Mia begged us, so we agreed to try it. The menu was awesome, and it had so many choices: dumplings, both steamed and pan-fried; marinated skewers of chicken and beef; scallion pancakes loaded with barbecued pork; and noodles with shrimp and mushrooms, and every kind of topping you could imagine!

I was studying the menu when Mia interrupted my thoughts. "Hey! I heard that the theme for the middle school Family Skating Party this year is Chinese New Year! Won't that be cool?"

I was dreading the Family Skating Party more than maybe I had ever dreaded anything. Clearly, I was alone in this.

"Awesome!" Katie agreed with Mia. "They could do such pretty red party decor with that theme, and it kind of ties in with Valentine's Day."

"Great food options with the Chinese theme, too. Much better than the Wild West theme last year," said Emma. "I hate eating ribs in public. So messy." She shook her head and laughed.

The other girls laughed too, and I imagined chasing the butterflies in my stomach around with a net and then whacking them!

"Alexis, is something wrong? You're being very quiet," Mia said.

"Yes," I answered grimly. "Don't you remember that I can't skate?"

"Wait, I thought you were going to take lessons!" said Emma.

3

I shook my head. "Didn't have time. I still stink. I think I might not go." I hated to miss a social opportunity where I might get to interact "in the real world" with Matt Taylor, Emma's brother and the crush of my life. But that was the primary reason I *wasn't* going. I couldn't stand the idea of being mortified in front of Matt. What if he saw that I was a bad skater? He's such a jock—he'd totally lose respect for me.

"Wait, *whaaaat*? What do you mean you might not go? You have to go!" said Emma just as we reached the front of the line.

"I don't want to discuss it," I said. "Let's order."

We pooled our money and ordered a bunch of different stuff to mix and match and share. The place was really busy, and it only had these long communal tables, so while we waited for our food to be ready, we split up and got busy scouting for people who were leaving.

Katie found a very tight spot for us after a few minutes, and Mia and Emma went to help save the seats while I returned to the counter to wait for our order. I saw my friend Ella Klinsky from school, and we waved and gestured to how crazy-busy the place was. Now that I was looking around, I could see that a lot of kids from school were here, sprinkled around. This Asian restaurant was popular with middle schoolers, that was for sure. I wondered how many of them could skate.

I was lost in thought, holding the little buzzer that they give you to tell you when your food is ready, twirling it in my hands and thinking about Valentine's Day. I know I am the no-nonsense type, but I am also kind of a sucker for all that romance stuff, believe it or not. I love the love songs on the radio, the romantic shows on TV, and my mom always decorates the table on Valentine's Day morning for breakfast. We have heart-shaped pancakes, and she gives us cards and candy and a little pink or red present, like cute red socks or something. It's a fun way to spice up blah old February, and I was looking forward to it.

Suddenly, someone very close behind me said, "Lexi?" I jumped and whirled around.

"Matt!" I cried. It was Matt Taylor, in the flesh! "Hi!" I felt myself blush hard (speaking of something red!), but I couldn't stop grinning.

"Hi!" he said, laughing. "Did I scare you?"

"Well, I don't exactly expect people to sneak up behind me in places like this and then speak directly into my ear!" I said, as if I was annoyed, but really I was just the opposite—thrilled!

"Sorry." He smiled, kind of shy. "Uh, what do you recommend here?"

I looked up at the menu, still smiling like a dope. "Well, we got . . ." And as I started to list our order, my buzzer went off, and I jumped again.

Matt was really laughing at me now. "A little jumpy today, are we?"

"Hungry, maybe!" I said. I handed my buzzer to the girl at the counter, and she handed me our tray. I looked down at it, and my mouth began to water. My friends were waiting, my food was ready, but I didn't want to leave. "Uh . . . where are you sitting?" I asked.

"I haven't found a spot yet. I'm solo. I'm sure I can just wedge in somewhere," he said, all casual. It was almost his turn to order.

"Well . . . come join us if you want. We can squeeze in," I said, wincing inwardly. Our spot was tiny. But I would happily squeeze in for him.

"Thanks. I'll look for you after I get my food."

I said good-bye and went to my friends, lowering the heavy tray onto the table. "Hey, Em, Matt's here," I said, like it was totally normal and cool.

She glanced up. "Oh yeah? He said he needed to go to the sporting goods store today, so I'm not surprised."

"He has no one to eat with," I said, doling out the food and perching on the end of the bench.

"Well, he can't sit here," Emma said grumpily. "There's no room!"

I grimaced and took a bite of a dumpling. It was delicious, and for a few minutes of bliss, I forgot all about Matt and ice-skating. "This is insane! Sooooo yummy!" I moaned.

We all traded containers and bites back and forth. Then I remembered about Matt, and I looked around. He had found a seat on his own near the end of another table. His back was to us and the seat across from him was empty. My heart clenched a little to see him eating all alone. I wanted to go join him, but I was nervous that my friends would get mad if I ditched them. Or worse, that if I went over there, someone would sit in the empty seat just as I reached it, and I'd be left standing there like a nerd—that would be so embarrassing. My palms began to sweat a little as I wrestled with the decision. *Should I stay or should I go?* I'd lost my appetite.

The other girls began discussing what they were going to get at the stationery store, and I sort of followed along distractedly as I stared at Matt's strong back and broad shoulders. I wondered if I should give him a valentine this year. The very thought made me feel sick to my stomach, but my dad always said you should do what you are afraid of doing, so maybe I should do it. Hmm.

"Okay, Alexis?" asked Emma.

"Huh? What?" I said, snapping out of my day-dream.

"The stationery store?"

"Oh. Uh . . . you know what? I'll just meet you there in a few minutes, okay? I . . . have one more thing to do." Did I really just lie to my friends for a boy? *Bad, bad Alexis!* But if they caught on, they didn't seem to mind, and they didn't ask any ques-tions (and I didn't offer any further explanation). We threw out our garbage—sorting everything into three cool-looking bins—one for food waste, one for paper stuff (which was most of it), and one for the few plastic cups and forks. Then they headed off and I doubled back to Matt's table. Luckily, Matt had bought a lot of food, so he was only about two thirds of the way finished.

"Hey," I said, all casual.

"Hey! Sit down!" He smiled and then wiped his mouth. "Awesome food, right?"

"Awesome," I agreed, perching in the mercifully still-empty seat across from him. "It was definitely time for a change around here. They needed to mix it up. I mean, how much Chinese food and pizza can they expect us to eat?"

Matt laughed and put his hand over his heart. "Hey, don't bust on my Panda Gardens."

I glanced across the food court at the Panda Gardens counter where everything was quiet. "You'd better get some soon, because I don't think they're going to be here much longer."

Matt gasped, all fake-horrified. "Take it back!"

I laughed. "I won't!" I put my hands to my mouth, like I was going to yell over to Panda Gardens, *Hey, PG, time to pack it in!*

Matt reached for my hands and tried to pry them from my face. I was laughing, and he was laughing, and I kept putting up my hands, so he would keep grabbing them away. It was funny, and it was soooo nice to feel his hands touch mine. He held my hands for one instant extra. We were both smiling, and then he said, "Well, I don't want to keep you from your friends."

"Oh, that's okay. They're in the stationery store. I have to go meet them in a minute. What are you up to now?"

Matt told me his errand list as we stood up together and went to recycle/throw away his stuff.

9

We found ourselves at the edge of the seating area, about to part ways. I was desperate to think of a way to prolong the encounter or to get him to touch my hands again, but I was distracted by his cuteness. My brain just wasn't working fast enough.

"So maybe I'll see you later?" I asked. "We're baking at your house today."

"Oh, cool. Okay. I'll be back after my practice. My dad is taking me straight from here, so . . ." It actually seemed like he wasn't ready to part yet either, which made me really psyched.

"Well . . . ," I stalled.

He grabbed my hand and gave it a squeeze. "Lay off Panda Gardens!" he said with a smile, and then he quickly dropped my hand and walked away without looking back.

I stood there grinning like an idiot. Then I whispered, "Thank you, Panda Gardens!" Promising myself to eat there sometime soon, I went to find my friends.

CHAPTER 2

Be Mine

At the stationery store, the other girls were in valentine heaven. Katie had gathered supplies to make homemade valentines—paper doilies, glitter, glue, and pink and red construction paper. Mia had an assortment of stuff she was going to use to make crafty little gifts—small white cardboard boxes to decorate with sticker gems and then fill with little candies. Emma had selected a fat stack of ready-made valentines.

I was still all googly eyed over Matt, but I didn't want to be weird about it around Emma, so I stayed off to the side and busied myself with the cards. I selected some regular ones for my parents and my older sister, Dylan, and then I continued my silent debate about buying one for Matt. I edged away from the family cards section ("For a wonderful Mother on Valentine's Day!") and into the funny greeting card area. I looked around to see if my friends were watching (they weren't), and then I quickly started rifling through the card selection, looking for one I might be able to give to Matt. They were all funny, but some were too forward, some assumed too much; many were way too lovey-dovey. I didn't know what to do!

What I needed was a card that said something like, "Hey, crush! I really like you, but if you don't like me like that, then pretend you never got this card. Oh, and don't tell anyone, either. Especially your sister, who is my best friend!"

Ha. Guess how many cards I found like that?

Sighing heavily, I circled up to the counter to pay for my three measly cards.

Mia sidled up next to me with her stuff. "All set?" she asked.

"I guess," I said. I glanced around to see where Emma was, and when I saw she was far across the store, I added, "I wanted to get something for Matt, but nothing here is really right."

Mia nodded in understanding. "Could you make him a valentine?"

I grimaced. "That seems so . . . serious. Like, a

12

lot of effort to put in, and what if he doesn't like me like that?"

Mia rolled her eyes and smiled. "Oh, I think he likes you like that. I wouldn't worry about it!"

"Really?" I couldn't hold back the huge grin that burst onto my face. "So maybe I should get him a card?"

Mia frowned thoughtfully. "Well . . . maybe it's better not to put anything in writing just yet. You know?"

It was now my turn to pay. I stepped forward. "So should I go back and get him some little gift?"

Mia furrowed her brow as she debated it.

"Next?" the lady at the counter called, a little annoyed. I had to pay.

I put down my stuff on the counter, and Mia was called to the register next to me.

She continued, "Why don't you get him something small . . . like, hmm. Flowers are too girlie. Too serious, anyway. Maybe a teddy bear?"

I shook my head. "Also a little girlie, I think?"

"Hey! Why don't you *say it with cupcakes*?" Mia suggested brightly. "You already know he loves cupcakes!"

"Who loves cupcakes?" said Katie, coming up behind us.

"Matt," I whispered.

Katie smiled. "Are you thinking of your valentine?"

I felt myself blush yet again. "Maybe," I said, turning to pay.

"How was your date?" asked Katie.

I whipped my head around. "What date?"

Katie was grinning. "Lunch at the mall?"

Busted!

"That wasn't a date! That was just . . . me not liking to see a friend eat alone." I shrugged, all casual, and took my bag from the cashier.

"Riiiiight!" Katie laughed. "That's why you didn't tell us where you were going!"

"It was a daaaaate!" singsonged Mia.

"Oh, shush!" I said, fake-annoyed but kind of pleased, too.

"Are you getting him something?" asked Katie.

"Well . . . I'm just debating. What do you think?" I asked, kind of hoping she'd say yes.

"Um, I don't know. Maybe wait and see if he gets *you* something?"

Oh.

Just then Emma arrived. "What's up? How did Matt like the new restaurant?"

"Oh, gosh. I'm sorry. I just . . ."

Emma smiled. "It's okay. You can be honest with us, though. You don't need to hide that you want to hang out with him. I'll let you know if it's cutting into our girl time," she said with a playful nudge.

I smiled goofily. "Thanks."

"Did you get him a card?" asked Emma, peering at my bag. She dumped her stuff on the counter and took out her wallet.

"No," I said.

"Good," Emma said, nodding firmly. "He's not really the mushy type."

O-kaaaay! I thought. *Now you tell me!*

"But Alexis *should* get him something, I think," protested Mia. "Or at least bake something for him. Maybe a bunch of cupcakes arranged on a platter into the shape of a heart?"

I winced. "That's a little psycho looking, I think."

"Food's not a bad idea," Emma agreed, taking her bag from the cashier. We headed to the exit. I felt myself hanging on her every word, like she was the expert on the subject of Matt Taylor.

"Like, what kind of food? Chocolates?" I asked eagerly.

"Nah." Emma shook her head. "He's not crazy about chocolate."

"Gummy worms?" I asked.

15

Emma smiled. "Do gummy worms really say romance?"

"True. What about cupcakes?"

Maybe Mia's idea wasn't so boring.

"Maybe . . . ," said Emma.

Suddenly, I felt a little annoyed. Like, why did Emma get all the power to decide what I should get Matt? He was only her brother. It wasn't like she knew him as a boyfriend or whatever. And why would Katie discourage me from doing something? Was she jealous because she and George Martinez are kind of on-and-off? Or did she really think I shouldn't get Matt something first, like I was being too pushy? Then again, maybe I should take Mia's advice and do something romantic, really let him know I like him like *that*. There were so many options! So many decisions! So many ways . . . to embarrass myself. I felt aggravated now.

"You know what? Thanks, everyone. I'll figure something out," I said, more cheerfully than I felt. My brain was swirling with ideas and opinions, and I was a little sick of discussing it. Valentines by committee are probably not a good idea.

"My only advice for you is: *less is more*," said Emma.

I huffed. "Thanks," I said. *Sort of,* I added in my

16

mind. I was kind of annoyed with Emma.

Mia threw me a sympathetic glance. "Hey," she said. "At least you like someone! I feel like I don't even know any boys!"

"Me, neither!" Katie agreed, at which point we all had to tease her about George.

"And I know too many!" Emma cried, who was always sick of living in boyland at her house.

"Poor Emma," said Mia, fake sympathetic.

We all laughed and then went out to meet Emma's mom for a ride home.

Back at the Taylors', I pulled my tablet from out of my bag and ducked into the bathroom, where I sat on the lid of the toilet and made a small list of the pros and cons of giving Matt a valentine of any sort.

Pros:

It would be nice of me.

He would probably like it.

Maybe it would take things to the next level.

Maybe he would give me something.

Maybe he would ask me out on a date.

Cons:

What if he doesn't like me like that?

What if Emma gets annoyed?
I am scared to go on a date.
What if he doesn't give me anything back?
What if he doesn't like what I give him?

I stared at the list. Yes or no? Do or die? Do *and* die (of embarrassment!)?

"Alexis?"

It was Emma calling me.

"In here!" I replied through the closed door.

"You okay? It's time to start baking!" she called.

"Coming!" I called, scrambling to tuck my tablet back in its sleeve.

I decided right then. One cupcake. That's all. That's what I'd give him. He could take it any way he wanted. One little cupcake. How much trouble could that be?

CHAPTER 3

Cool Dude

I put my tablet in its sleeve on top of my messenger bag, which I'd put on a chair in the Taylors' front hall, where it would be out of the way of the baking mess in the kitchen. Then I went into the kitchen to get going on the cupcakes.

Mia was already making the batter and Emma was putting the liners in the pans. Katie was putting the decorations into little bowls. I decided to make the frosting.

"Everyone done with their homework?" I asked.

Mia groaned. "Of course not! It's only Saturday!"

"I do mine on Fridays. Why ruin the weekend with it hanging over your head?" I asked.

"Why ruin your Friday?" said Mia. "I am just so psyched to dump my book bag and not even think about school on Fridays. Or Saturdays. Seriously, Alexis!"

"We have a lot of work these days," Emma said kind of miserably.

"You just have to stay on top of it. Chunk it. Bite-size," I said. Stuff like that is so obvious to me. "Also, plan ahead and do a little every day."

"I don't work well like that," Katie said with a shrug. "I'm all about the deadline. Up till the last minute."

"Me too," agreed Mia.

I shuddered. "I can't think of anything worse than leaving things till the last minute. It totally stresses you out. And for what? It's not like people do better work under a deadline."

"I do," said Mia.

"Humph. That's just what you *think*."

"Wait, speaking of deadlines, let's talk about this skating thing," said Emma. "Can't you take just one lesson this week after school? The party's not till Friday night."

"I have something every day after school this week," I said.

"Tomorrow?" suggested Emma.

"Maybe. I don't know. They're probably already booked."

"Wait, what about Thursday? We have a half day for Teacher Improvement Conferences," said Katie.

"Well, maybe I could try for Thursday. I have to ask my mom. It's Teacher *Development*, by the way," I corrected her.

Katie giggled and shrugged. "Same thing."

"Okay. Hey, Alexis, in the meantime . . . You're all about research." Mia shrugged. "Maybe you could look up some skating stuff online or something."

Hmm. Not a bad idea. "Maybe," I said.

"Listen. You just have to come to the skating party! You know, Matt will be there. . . ." Emma said tantalizingly.

"That's what I'm afraid of," I muttered. "I don't know. Let me think about it. Now, come on—let's focus on the task at hand!" I said, like a strict parent. The others got the hint and we switched topics to discuss our process for today.

Katie had a cute idea for Valentine's Day cupcakes, and we were giving it a shot. First, you bake a thin red velvet sheet cake. Then, after the red cake cools, you use a very small heart-shaped cookie cutter to stamp out little red cake hearts. (Katie had made the cake at home last night and dropped it off at the Taylors' this morning, so we wouldn't waste any time.) Then you bake vanilla cupcakes. When you fill the liners with the white batter, you sink a spongy little heart into each cup, standing it on its end. When the cupcake is all done, it has a secret red cakey heart, buried inside. Katie had e-mailed us a link to the online photo, and we all thought it was adorable. I couldn't wait to see how they came out.

If it was a fail, we'd just frost the white cupcakes in a cute pink frosting and add the decorations we'd be using either way—pink sparkly sugar, Red Hots, little piped red gel frosting hearts on top. Adorable, still. . . .

Katie busied herself with cutting out the hearts, and Mia—who is very good with her hands—stood them in the batter. We got the cupcakes into the oven and then watched TV for a bit while they baked. Naturally, *Ballroom Dancing* was running a Valentine's Day marathon, and it was great. Everyone was dancing to romantic songs, and people were in pink and red costumes, and everything was sappy and lovey-dovey. It made me think of Matt, even though we have rarely danced together, and certainly not ballroom style—nor do we ever dress in pink and red together. But still . . . it reminded me of Matt. At least the romantic part.

I didn't want the show to end, but after the

baking timer called, and Katie set out the cakes to cool for a bit, it was time to get hopping. At this point, Matt was due home, so I was getting excited and nervous. How would I decorate my cupcake valentine for him? Would it be too much that there was a little heart in it? Was that too pushy? *Ugh! Love is stressful!*

I needed to help get all the cupcakes we were selling done first, so I focused on that and busied myself slathering on pink frosting. Mia was in charge of artfully sprinkling on edible pink sparkles, and then Katie would pipe on the red heart. Emma would carefully place some Red Hots on each one.

In their candy-cane–striped papers, the finished product looked adorable! Almost too cute to eat.

I slathered the frosting on the final cupcake and licked a splotch of it from my finger. Yum. With my work done, I could focus on the cupcake for Matt.

Should I make it very fancy, like I had put a lot into it, like *Hello, valentine, I slaved over this just for you?* Or kind of plain and off-hand, like, *Hey, we had an extra cupcake, so you can have it?* Worse, I had to ask the others if they minded if I took a cupcake for myself.

"Hey, guys? Would you mind . . . uh . . . Is it okay if I take one of these? I can repay the club. I just want one, please. I'll pay the club back tomorrow."

Emma looked up and raised her eyebrows suspiciously at me.

Uh-oh. I gulped. I didn't want to have to explain it to her, in case she vetoed it, saying it was too "mushy" or a bad idea. I didn't have another plan, and I'd be back to square one.

"Sure," she said. "Are you eating it?"

"Oh, no . . ." I waved my hand breezily and gave a forced laugh. "Just . . ." I let the word trail off. I couldn't think of anything to say and didn't want to lie to her.

Mia smirked at me and said, "Go for it." She obviously knew why I needed it.

Katie said, "Oh, Alexis, you never have to ask us for a cupcake. And you certainly don't need to pay for it, silly!"

"Thanks." I took the largest, fluffiest one I could find, and then I set about decorating it as best I could. I did a flowery petal design with the red gel frosting, and then I filled in the "leaves" with pink sparkly sugar and added a Red Hot at the center. It actually looked really good.

Katie leaned over my shoulder and said, "Wow! Who knew you had such decorating skills?"

I felt faint with relief. "Is it good? Do you think?"

"Awesome," said Mia, coming over to look.

Emma glanced over. "Cute!" she said, kind of casually. Hmm.

I set it aside on a napkin, waiting for just the right moment to run it upstairs and leave it on Matt's desk. We took a photo of all the party cupcakes for our website and then packed them to be delivered to the luncheon the next day.

Just then we heard a car pull in the driveway. Emma groaned. "Here come the boys. Thank goodness we finished packing everything up or there'd be nothing left!"

Emma's little brother, Jake, came bolting through the back door. "I gotta go to the bathroom, and Dad needs help! Save me a cupcake!" he yelled and then raced upstairs.

"None left!" Emma called after him.

Then Emma went out to see what her dad needed, and I knew my moment had come. I grabbed the napkin and the cupcake and then bolted up the stairs to Matt's room, narrowly missing Jake as the bathroom door closed behind him. I felt like I was invading Matt's privacy, so I didn't even look around his room, really. (Well, okay, just a little bit. And I was thrilled to spy a photo of all of us in costumes from Halloween on his bulletin board. Maybe he did care!) I placed the napkin on the center of his blotter, where he wouldn't miss it, grabbed a felt-tip marker from his pen jar, and wrote "Happy Valentine's Day. From, Alexis" on it. ("Love, Alexis" seemed really too much, so I didn't do that.) I placed the cupcake on the napkin, turned on my heels, and raced downstairs. I wasn't even gone thirty seconds. Phew.

Soon after I returned, Emma and Matt trudged from the mudroom carrying armloads of firewood for their woodstove, and the rest of us raced to help. I'd just made it! But now . . . I was too scared to look Matt in the eye! What have I done? What if he thought the cupcake meant I loved him? So what if it does? Ugh! I considered running back upstairs to grab it, but I'd certainly be caught. Now I was stuck.

We passed each other in the doorway, and I looked up and smiled a little. He smiled back. "Hey!" he said brightly, like nothing was weird at all. And it wasn't. *Yet!* Oh boy. I felt my face begin to burn. I was embarrassed. But a part of me was also excited. Like maybe this would take things to the next level, whatever that was. Or maybe he would give me something too! Maybe he already had something for me, right this very minute, that he got at the mall! That would be so awesome!

The firewood was inside in no time, and we girls went back to the den. Matt disappeared upstairs to shower, and I waited, on pins and needles, for him to come downstairs to say thanks for the cupcake. Would he do it right away, before his shower, or wait till he was clean? Would he do it in front of the others (embarrassing!), or would he find a way to pull me aside? My palms were actually sweating, and I fluctuated between mortification and excitement. A few minutes went by, and he didn't come down. Okay, so he ate it, and now he's showering. I craned my neck to see if I could hear the water running, but there was nothing.

Jake appeared in the doorway with a funny grin on his face.

Emma looked over at him. "What's up, Jakey?" She looked at him again and narrowed her eyes suspiciously. "Did you touch our cupcakes in the kitchen?" she demanded.

Jake shook his head vehemently. "No! I didn't even see them there!" He looked like he was telling the truth, but there was definitely more than met the eye. We all looked at him for an extra few seconds, and then he yelled, "I'm not lying, Emmy!" and took off out of the room.

"Weird," Emma said, shaking her head and turning back to the movie that started playing.

Mia turned out the lights and an oldie but goodie began to play—*Casablanca*. I usually don't care for old black-and-white movies, but I couldn't help from getting swept away by the love story a little bit. Suddenly, I noticed almost half an hour had slipped by, and no Matt. I told the others I was going to the bathroom, and no need to pause the movie for me, and then I went into the downstairs hallway to crane my neck again and listen.

Silence.

No shower running, no music playing, no footsteps moving around upstairs. Weird.

Feeling deflated, I happened to glance down at my tablet on the chair as I went back to the den. It had a clump of pink frosting on it. That was weird. Had I touched it after I frosted the cupcakes? I didn't think so.

I went back into the den. "Anyone get frosting on my tablet? I don't care. . . . Just, it's in a weird place."

Everyone was engrossed in the movie, so they looked at me, shook their heads, and turned back to the TV. This day was turning out oddly, and I was not happy about it. How could Matt walk past a gorgeous cupcake valentine on his desk and not even come downstairs to thank me? He always made a big deal of it when we gave him cupcakes—swooning over them and saying how good they are. He must've seen it! He must've eaten it! Right?

At first I was annoyed, like how rude can someone be? But then doubt became stronger than annoyance, and I began to realize I'd made a mistake.

Duh!

Matt didn't like me like that. I was just a friend. Giving him a cupcake valentine was creepy and pushy, and he was too weirded out to even come back downstairs, so he was hiding up there. How could I be so dumb? Mortification—much deeper than embarrassment—took over. I began to sweat and my face burned, and I was just itching to get out of there. I couldn't even hear what they were saying in the movie, I was so distracted. Finally, my nerves got the better of me and I hopped up.

"Guys, gotta go. I'm sorry. I just . . . remembered I have some more work to do for the Future Business Leaders of America summit, so . . ."

"Wait! Why? Hit pause!" said Emma to Mia, who had the remote. "Why do you have to go? Weren't we maybe thinking about a sleepover?"

29

Ugh. I knew they would be suspicious because I never forget about work, but I couldn't even imagine having to spend the night there, not when I felt like this! Not when he was here too! And my big, beautiful cupcake just hanging out there, unacknowledged!

I had to go. "Oh, not with this . . . I . . . can't. I'm so sorry. Rain check. Thanks! Talk to you guys later."

And I ducked out of the room, grabbed my tablet and messenger bag, and then my coat, and raced out the door.

I never saw Matt again.

That day, I mean.

CHAPTER 4

Sweet Home

Well, actually, it really did feel like I never saw him again. On Sunday I just camped out in my room. I checked e-mail and texts a million times to see if he'd maybe had a change of heart or even if he wanted to get in touch to tell me to stay away. But there was nothing. And I was too distracted to do much else. It was boring and stressful all at the same time.

My mom came up to my room a couple of times that morning to try to chat or entice me downstairs. I kept saying I was working, but it was obvious I wasn't doing much. Later, I ate my lunch and went back up to clean my closet (already neat) and sulk.

The third time she came up, she asked, "Honey,

what's the matter? And please don't say nothing is wrong. I know something is bothering you."

I sighed. How could I begin to explain it all to her, and without making myself sound even worse?

She sat on my bed and folded her arms and legs. "I am not leaving until you tell me why you're holed up in here all day. It's unhealthy, and it's not like you. Spill it!" She wiggled her foot and waited.

Hmm. I was so embarrassed, honestly, that I couldn't even face telling my own mom. I'd have to just tell her part of it.

"I just was thinking about Valentine's Day tomorrow and not having a valentine."

"*Oh!*" said my mom. I could tell she was hugely relieved. She'd probably thought I'd failed a test or something. For her, this was not a big deal. "Okay. So you mean like a boy valentine?"

"Yes, Mother," I said in annoyance.

"Sorry. Okay. Of course. Well, do you still like Matt Taylor? He'd make a nice valentine."

"Mom, it's not like you just decide who you like, and then they're your valentine!"—even though that was exactly what I'd done!—"You have to have cause to believe that the valentine will be well-received and that you'll get one in return!"

My mom smiled, and it looked like she was

going to laugh for a second, but then she got all serious again. "Well, I don't think you should put too much stock in Valentine's Day," said my mom. "It's a holiday made up by candymakers and greeting card manufacturers just to sell junk. Of course, as a marketing idea, it is really rather clever—anyone who doesn't participate feels left out, so it has created a kind of urgency whereby people must buy their products or suffer, as you are doing right now." She is the CFO of a company so is always thinking of the business angle of things. (Ahem, like me.)

I didn't want this to turn into a business meeting, so I pressed on. "But I do feel left out. I want someone to like me."

"I like you! Daddy and Dylan like you!" my mom protested, grinning. She knew that wasn't what I meant.

"Mom. That's not what I meant. And anyway, Dylan does not like me."

"Okay, you're right," she agreed, joking. She continued, "Listen, all kidding aside, I think you are too young to be worried about this, number one. There are more important things to life at your age—namely, yourself! And here's a little secret: Most adults don't even make that big a deal of

Valentine's Day. It's kind of an silly holiday. Number two, since you don't have a significant other in your life, you actually don't *need* to worry about it. If you did have a boyfriend or something, you could worry about what to do for Valentine's Day, but you don't, so don't worry about it!"

At this, I burst into tears.

"Sweetheart!" my mom cried, standing and coming to put an arm around my shoulders. "I am so sorry!"

"I wish I *did* have a boyfriend!" I wailed.

She hugged me and patted my back and whispered comforting words, and although it was nice, it didn't actually help. The only thing that would have helped was Matt texting/calling/typing to say he loved the cupcake. That's all! Not even "I loved the cupcake and want to go on a date with you." Not even that!

But there was nothing.

"Listen, Alexis. I'm going to make your favorite chicken fajitas for dinner tonight. I'm going to the store in half an hour. Just understand, you are at a point in your life where family and friends come first. Boys will come along in due time, and you will be beating them off with a stick, trust me. But for now, pull yourself together. Get yourself downstairs

34

and call Emma or Mia or Katie, and make a plan to do something fun this afternoon. Ideally, something with fresh air and exercise. You're done with all of your homework, right?"

As if she really needed to ask that. I nodded.

"Okay, then. If you need a ride anywhere, I can take you on my way to the grocery store. Chop, chop!" She kissed the top of my head again and left the room.

I grabbed a tissue and blew my nose and dried my eyes. Then I took a deep breath. I sent a group text out to see what the Cupcakers were doing after lunch and if anyone wanted to go skating or anything.

It only took two seconds for Katie and Mia to reply that they wished they could but they were doing their homework.

Shortly after, Emma replied that she was baby-sitting Jake, so she couldn't go skating, but did I want to come over?

Sighing deeply, I replied, "N. Thx." And pressed send.

She replied that she strongly encouraged me to use the time for a skating lesson. I sulked for a minute, then impulsively, I picked up the phone and called the skating rink where the Family Skating

Party was always held. The lady who answered was nice and said I could have a one-hour lesson with a junior pro at three o'clock for forty dollars. I had the money myself saved up from Cupcake Club stuff so I didn't have to ask for it, which was nice. I booked it and then went to coordinate a ride there and back with my mom.

My mom dropped me at the rink while she went to the grocery store, and she said if she finished early, she'd come watch me. I privately hoped the checkout lines were long because I did *not* need an audience! I closed the car door and headed in through the gate.

The skating rink was actually a tennis club in the summer, but every winter they built a really big rink with boards and chillers to keep the ice cold, and they had nighttime lighting (little twinkly lights in addition to the big floodlights) and music on the PA system, and it opened each year from early December to March. Inside the little clubhouse was a roaring fire surrounded by huge sofas, and a skate rental counter, and a snack bar that sold homemade soup and hot chocolate and plastic bags of popcorn, among other rinkside staples. (Hey, another possible Cupcake Club client!) The whole place felt cozy, like a ski lodge, and if I had been an even remotely decent skater, I would have spent a great deal of time here every winter. But, ahem, I wasn't.

At the counter, a cheerful-looking woman stood sharpening ice skates.

"Hi, um, I'm Alexis Becker? I called earlier about the lesson?" I felt my palms growing sweaty just thinking about it.

"Oh, right! Hi, honey." She smiled, and I tried to relax. She turned off the skate-sharpening machine and went over to the register. "That will be forty dollars, please. You're with Sasha today. She's very good. I'm sure you'll have fun."

I gulped in nervousness. "Okay," I said. "I'm sure." She might as well have been telling me I was going to have fun at the dentist.

"And you'd like to rent skates, too, right? It's free with the lesson."

"Yes, please." I handed her the forty dollars, kind of wincing. I hate spending money in general, but spending it on things I don't really want is about the worst.

"Shoe size?"

"Nine and a half," I whispered. My big feet always embarrass me.

She nodded and then went to get the skates.

As I waited, I glanced around the dining area and then did a double-take.

My heart dropped.

Seated at a table in the snack bar were Olivia Allen and the other members of the BFC, or the Best Friends Club. My *least* favorite people at school. They were the kind of girls who would snub you in public, scheme to get a boy's attention, speak to you only if other people from school were nowhere in sight (like if you ran into one of them at an airport with your family and your moms knew each other), laugh if you did something embarrassing at school, and so on. You get the idea. The last thing on earth I needed right now was for them to watch me take a beginner's skating lesson.

I considered fleeing right then and there.

But the lady reappeared with the navy blue skates in my size and handed them to me with such a cheerful "Have fun, honey!" that there was nothing for me to do but take them and skulk in a daze over to a bench in the dressing area to put them on. My lesson with Sasha would start in ten minutes. She was probably just like the BFC— stylish and beautiful and too cool for me—and the whole hour would be torture. Oh, why did I do this so impulsively? I would have given anything for another Cupcaker to be there right then.

The skates fit, but they felt heavy and awkward. I didn't dare look back around the rental counter to see where the BFC girls were. I stayed frozen in my spot in the hopes they would stay at their table and I could slink out onto the ice without them seeing me. I had ten minutes to kill.

I pulled my hat low over my forehead, tucked my chin into my zipped-up ski jacket, pulled on my mittens, and slouched against the wall until it was time.

Unfortunately, everyone was getting ready to hit the ice for a four o'clock session, and it wasn't even a minute when the BFC swarmed the benches around me to get ready for what turned out to be their synchronized skating team practice. How it was possible for Olivia to ID me solely by seeing the one exposed inch of my face, I will never know, but she said, "Alexis! What are *you* doing here?" in a loud, phony voice when she arrived. "Girls, look who's here!"

They all looked at me, and a couple of them kind of nodded, but that was it. I wouldn't have expected more. Most of us weren't exactly on a first name basis.

"Are you trying out for our team?" Olivia asked, then she shot the other girls a look and they all giggled.

"Nope. Just getting some exercise," I said.

"Nothing like exercising in the great outdoors!" chirped Olivia.

"Uh-huh," I agreed.

She looked down at my skates. "Are those... rentals?" she asked, wrinkling her nose in distaste.

"Yup," I said, looking away.

"Gross. How can you put your feet in those things after they've been all sweated up by strangers?" She shuddered. "I could *never*!"

I shrugged. I hadn't really thought about that aspect. The skates were dry when I put them on. "I forgot mine," I lied. I tried not to think about strangers' sweat.

"Well, then, have your mom come bring them!" she insisted.

"She's . . . out."

"I would have canceled, then," said Olivia with one last look of disgust.

I should have, I thought.

She and the others began peeling off their warm-up suits, until they were each in an adorable, flirty, little colored dress and tan stockings that went clear down over their white figure skates and made their legs look long and their feet look tiny. They all looked like Olympians, of course. I guessed that was the point.

"Oooh, Bella!" Olivia squealed. "Let's see you in the new teal!"

Bella stood and modeled a tiny dress, and everyone looked to Olivia for her verdict before they said anything.

Olivia stood and cased Bella, stalking her in a circle like she was admiring a statue at a museum.

Finally, Olivia said, "It looks gorgeous on you! I love it!" The other girls all nodded. Their leader had spoken.

Bella heaved a sigh of relief and a huge grin spread across her face as Olivia turned her attention back to me.

"So who's your lesson with?" she asked, bending to tighten her skates.

"Sasha?" I said unenthusiastically. I didn't want her to think I thought Sasha was some awesome person since I'd never even met her.

But Olivia stood bolt upright. "Really?" she asked, her eyes wide.

"Um . . . yeah?" *Is this good news or bad?* I wondered.

"Wow," Olivia said breathlessly. And then "Girls," she called to her team. "Alexis is having a lesson with *Sasha*." There was heavy meaning implied in the way she said Sasha's name, like they all would understand how significant a fact this was. However, I was totally in the dark.

They all said "Wow," or some version of it, that implied awe, but again, I couldn't tell if it was good or bad.

I didn't want to let on that I was clueless, so I just sat there and waited for Olivia to say more, to give me an indication of how I should react. She was looking at me in kind of a funny way, eyeing my blue skates, my outfit, and then kind of shaking her head like she was confused.

"So, how did *you* end up with Sasha?" she asked casually.

"I called and that's who they gave me." I shrugged, like I couldn't help it.

"Huh," said Olivia. "Oh! Here she comes!"

She was looking over my shoulder. Olivia scrambled to stand up straight, so I did too. And then I turned around to search for someone—I don't know who I was expecting—but when I looked, I had to look down. Way down. Sasha was tiny, but so beautiful, like a porcelain doll. She had jet-black hair, white skin, full red lips, and long, long black eyelashes framing sky blue eyes. She was wearing a red warm-up suit that was form-fitting, and I could see how athletic and lithe she was. Her white skates were pristine, and everything about her was perfect, from her tight ponytail to the tiny gold studs in each ear.

I smiled nervously and glanced at Olivia for some kind of guidance, but Olivia was staring openmouthed at Sasha.

Um, okay.

Sasha spoke first, and she had a beautiful accent that sounded like she might be Russian. "Hello! You are Alexis? I am Sasha." She put out her tiny hand to shake mine, and I felt like a polar bear extending a huge paw. I had to take off my mitten, and still my hand looked huge in comparison.

"Hello," I said meekly, and I smiled again. She didn't smile back, but she wasn't unfriendly. Just very, very serious.

"Shall we go?" Sasha said, gesturing to the rink.

I gulped and nodded, terrified. She began to walk, and I followed her.

"Hi, Sasha!" Olivia called desperately after us.

Sasha half turned and nodded in Olivia's direction.

"Hey, Sasha!" all the other synchronized skaters called eagerly.

But Sasha didn't turn around again. With perfect posture and elegance, she walked to the door in her skates, pushed it open, and held it for me. I went through and she followed.

Outside, as we walked down the rubber-padded ramp to the rink entrance she shivered and said, "Those girls are always so mean. I hope they are not your friends."

And right then and there, I relaxed. I knew things were going to be okay!

"No. They are not my friends. Not at all," I said triumphantly.

Then we edged our way onto the ice, and I promptly stumbled and fell down.

It was going to be a long hour.

CHAPTER 5

You Rock

Sasha was a tiny seventeen-year-old Ukrainian on the pro track, and because she was organized and driven, like me, we hit it off immediately, despite the fact most people who are great skaters (and drop-dead gorgeous) make me insanely jealous. Her family had emigrated from Ukraine the year before, and Sasha was being homeschooled, so she could train with a famous figure skating coach an hour away. She had been on the Ukrainian Junior National Team for figure skating and would be trying out for the US skating team when her green card came through, hopefully soon. Meanwhile, besides her training and schooling, she gave lessons around the area to earn extra cash to pay her trainer. I got all this in the first couple of minutes of our lesson. She was very chatty and friendly.

When I fell down immediately, she was patient. She said, "Okay, so you are beginner."

I had to laugh, I was so embarrassed. Plus, it was funny how she stated the obvious in her deadpan way. "Yes." I said, shaking my head. "I am a beginner." And then I couldn't get up. I had to flip onto my hands and knees like a baby and scrabble up as Sasha tried to lift me. She was much stronger than you would have thought for someone her size. Must've been all that Olympic training.

My legs flailed a little, but when Sasha whispered, "Quick, they come!" I knew who she meant and was immediately grateful. That was all it took to motivate me. I grasped for the edge of the rink and pulled myself into a steady upright position. As the synchronized skaters clomped down the ramp, stepped over the threshold to the ice, and then went gliding like a flock of multicolored swans across a frozen pond, I stood stock-still and watched them go. Only Olivia turned her head to glance back at us as she went by. And her look seemed almost wistful, like I had something she wanted. That would be a first!

As soon as they reached the far end of the rink, Sasha said, "I am sorry. I did not mean to scare you.

But I did not want you down on the ground as they passed."

"I appreciate it," I said.

"So you want to skate, why? For exercise?" she asked.

I explained about the Family Skating Party that was being held on Friday. I didn't mention Matt. I didn't really know Sasha, and I felt too shy. "I just want to not make a fool of myself," I said. *That about covers it, anyway,* I thought.

"Okay," Sasha began, nodding. "So we will take it from beginning. The ice is slippery. Your skates are not. You are in control of how you move, and you will need every muscle. You can ski?" she asked, tipping her head to the side.

I nodded.

"Good. Is very much like skiing," she said. "We will push skates: right foot out to right, left foot out to left. Beginners always thinking it is for-ward backward, like shush, shush." She moved her feet in a straight line, forward and backward, like she was trying to carve the ice. Then she grabbed hold of the side of the rink and showed me what she meant about skiing. "You know when you are on the flat terrain in your skis and you have to get to the lift? You must push the skis out to the side?

47

Is same motion. Let's see you try it."

She let go of the side of the rink and pushed away in a perfect, graceful arc. "Here. Give me your hands. I will take you for quick ride to give you a taste. Just relax. I will not let you fall. Now with mean girls here, we have motivation to stay upright. Is good." She cracked a small smile for the first time and I smiled back. *Yes. Is good motivation,* I thought in a Russian accent.

Sasha took me by the hands and, skating backward, pulled me along on a brisk ride. The wind felt nice on my face, and I could see the appeal of being able to skate well. I couldn't believe she was doing this all backward. Yikes.

"Bend knees a little, chest up, keep skates parallel. Head up," she instructed, looking back over her shoulder to make sure we wouldn't crash into anyone. "Can you feel the ice through the blades? Is little bit bumpy, no? But feel how good is the glide. Relaxing. Beautiful. Fun. You like it?"

I had to smile. When someone else was doing all the work, ice-skating wasn't half bad. "Yes," I agreed.

"Good. Now we will teach you to do. Skating is all angles. You like math?" Sasha asked, bringing us back to a stop where we had started.

"I love it," I said.

She smiled that rare flash of a smile, and nodded. "Good. Think of blade as upside-down U shape." She cupped her hand and showed me what she meant. "Inside edge is here, outside edge here." She indicated her thumb for the inside, and then the rest of her fingers for the outside. "You will work from inside edge. Starting position is feet side by side, shoulder-width apart. Angle toes in tiny bit; maybe twenty degrees. Bend knees." She bounced a little in place, and I lined up my skates, bent my knees, and copied her.

"Good." She nodded, pleased.

I looked down at my feet in the clunky skates to admire my work.

"Keep chest up, eyes ahead. No looking down at toes!" she commanded.

I whipped my head up and looked straight ahead.

"Yes! Now we will do one push, then glide. Hands out to sides for balancing. Put all weight on left foot. Tip right toe out at forty-five-degree angle, then push out to side like flat skiing. Will start you moving."

I did as I was told and pushed out to the side, leaving my weight on my left foot. I wobbled as I began to move, but with my eyes straight ahead, I could see the synchronized girls floating across the ice and ordered myself to stay upright rather than fall.

Sasha was very happy. She clapped her tiny hands. "Yes! Very good student. Do again. Keep pushing just with right foot. Like skateboard. Is okay for now."

I kept pushing myself along, balancing on the left foot.

"Wait! Stop!" commanded Sasha. She gently held my arm to stop me from moving, and then she skated me over to the wall. "Skates are too loose. Toes must move, ankles must be rigid. Let me retie." She bent and fiddled with each skate, yanking the laces so hard at the top that I gasped. She looked up. "Sorry. But if skates are not right, then they become enemy working against you, not friend helping."

I giggled. "I need friends helping. That's for sure." I pictured the Cupcakers and wished again that they were here. A group lesson would be fun, but maybe we'd laugh too much.

Sasha stood and brushed the ice off her knees. "Okay. Begin again. Weight on left foot. Angle right toe out . . ."

"Forty-five degrees!" I chirped. Numbers were always easy for me to remember.

"Very good memory! Chest up. Push!"

I did it and went gliding again. It felt so good to be moving along under my own steam, even if I was slow and wobbly.

We were working our way around the outer edge of the rink and began to draw closer to the synchronized girls. They were working on a routine now, and skating all together in rows. It was pretty impressive, actually, and they were beautiful skaters: smooth and fluid and very, very steady. I was gliding well on my one foot, but I looked like a total dork with my arms out. As we drew nearer, I decided I'd make it look like I knew what I was doing, so I put my arms down at my sides and kept doing my dumb push with my right foot and glide on my left. At first it felt okay with my arms down. Sasha and I were silent as we drew alongside the girls. They all turned to look at us during a pause in their routine, and as we passed them, my head turned to look back, and it threw me off balance. I lifted my arms to steady myself, but it was too late. My toes began going in different directions, and my legs got all out of control, and I started to frantically windmill my arms to keep from falling.

I went down fast and hit the ice hard on my butt, right in front of all of them. For a moment I wished I could have just disappeared.

I wasn't down more than two seconds before I felt Sasha's strong arms flip me up onto my feet, and she began pulling me away from the girls. They were all looking at me in shock, their jaws hanging open.

Haven't you ever seen a beginner before? I wanted to yell, but if I opened my mouth, I knew I might cry. I could just imagine how they must be laughing now and shaking their heads at my clumsiness.

Sasha pulled me to the other end of the rink and stopped with a big spray of ice shavings, breathless. "We will not go down there again," she said. "We can stay down here to work, okay?" She tipped her head kindly and looked at me. "Are you okay?"

I nodded, willing myself not to cry.

Sasha gave a huge angry huff and pulled back to lean against the boards. She crossed her arms and said quietly, without looking at me, "Those girls, they make fun of my accent—they laugh at how small I am. They are not friendly, not nice. Is okay. I am not here to make friends. But still . . . I am not happy here in beginning, and they are part of problem. Now is better. I see how they are, I avoid them. I don't know why people are like that. Back home, other skaters help one another. Is like family. Skating is happy for me, but not so much when they are here." She rocked back and forth on her skates, and two red blotches appeared on her cheeks. "So now we must make you excellent skater. No falling near those girls again, okay?"

I took a deep breath. However mean they were to me, at least I had lots of other friends, and I didn't need to see those mean girls every time I went to do something I loved. "Okay," I agreed. "I'm sorry they were mean to you. I . . . actually think they're intimidated by you." I realized it was true as I said it.

Sasha gave a little laugh and a shrug. "Funny way to show respect. In my country, we are humble. We ask people we respect for help. Now. We work again!" She pushed off from the wall, and we began the lesson in earnest, with renewed vigor. I understood we both had something to prove to those synchronized skaters, and we needed each other in order to do it.

Sasha showed me how to push and glide using both feet, transferring my weight from one foot to the other by angling the center point of my chest over my toes, alternating from side to side. I'd bend and push, then glide . . . bend and push, then glide.

It began to feel good. I kept my arms out to the sides for most of the time, but sometimes I'd lower them, just to look normal for a minute, and Sasha would tsk-tsk me. She said I wasn't quite ready and "would cause to falling."

We spent fifteen minutes on learning to stop, which I hadn't realized was so important until I learned how to glide. Sasha had me hold the wall and work on my snowplow stop, turning one toe in at a forty-five-degree angle and pushing hard on the inner edge of the blade.

By the end of the lesson, Sasha and I were chatting and having a great time. Math was her favorite subject too, and she wanted to be a business major in college, so we had plenty to chat about as I skated (yes, me!). It almost helped to talk while we did it because then I wasn't *too* focused on my feet.

At the very end, with five minutes left, I asked if she would show me something cool that she could do. The ice had emptied out, and there were only a few lone skaters still out, plus the girl gang in their corner. The late afternoon had darkened into evening, and the spotlights were humming brightly overhead.

Sasha looked shy all of a sudden. "Is still your lesson time. Plus, I don't know if there's space."

"Please? Just a little jump or something?"

Sasha looked at me with her head tipped, then suddenly she took off like a shot, skating hard around the outside edge of the rink at breakneck speed. The power in her strides was astonishing! She could glide on just one push for half the rink, and fast! She did two fast laps of the rink, and as she came around the final lap, she jumped about three feet into the air, did a double turn, and then landed in that figure skating way, with one leg extended back perfectly and her arms flung out to the sides in a perfect line. Then she stopped in front of me with a sharp *shuss!* Her eyes were shining happily.

"Oh, Sasha! That was incredible!" I cried, clapping.

She smiled. "Thank you. You can watch rest on YouTube. Clip from Russian Nationals is on there."

"Oh, I will! I can't wait! I've never seen someone do that up close and in real life. I can't believe it!" It was like she was another kind of being—more than human. That proficiency and power was awe-inspiring.

Just then, the synchronized team came gliding by, skirts flapping.

"Pretty turn, Sasha!" said Olivia, all worshipful.

Sasha nodded in acknowledgment of the compliment but didn't say anything. They all passed by, and we were silent for a minute.

"Sasha, I can't begin to thank you. That was so fun, and I feel so much better now."

"Yes, was fun. You are good athlete. Very graceful. You can do this. Just little more practice, and no one will know you just started."

We exited the rink carefully, me clutching the side of the rink like a drowning swimmer, but at least I didn't fall. Clomping up the ramp, I admitted, "There's a boy I like, who's going to be at the skating party on Friday, so . . ."

Sasha turned to grin at me. "Is even better motivation than mean girls!"

I grinned back. "I know."

My mom was inside the clubhouse when we got to the top, and I introduced Sasha, and they chatted as I untied my skates and returned them. Leaving, we said good-bye to Sasha, who had another lesson waiting, and impulsively, I gave her a hug. She returned it with a tight squeeze.

"Good luck, Alexis. Come back and visit, okay? You will do great on Friday," she said, holding me by my shoulders and giving me a tiny shake.

"Thanks. It was a blast. I'll see you soon," I said.

Walking out, my mom and I fell in with Olivia Allen, which was a major buzzkill.

"You are so lucky," said Olivia, awestruck. "How did you ever get her to work with you? She's like . . . a professional. An Olympian."

I looked Olivia straight in the eye. "I just called up, I told you. But you know what? She's really nice and really lonely. You should try talking to her sometime." And then I headed to our car, with Olivia still standing there in the parking lot, biting her lip and thinking.

As soon as I got home, I brought my laptop down to the kitchen, so I could search Sasha's skating videos and show them to my mom while she made the fajitas. In the Russian Nationals video, Sasha danced in a pale blue velour costume with long sleeves, and she was incredible. Graceful and fast, with tons of tricks and no falls. I would have given her a perfect score if I was the judge, but the video didn't show the result.

"What a lovely girl," said my mom, watching over my shoulder. "So talented, so hardworking."

"And so nice," I agreed.

The rest of the evening wound down in a boring Sunday fashion that had me longing for Monday morning. Though the only valentines I had to look forward to were from my *mother*, at least it was something. But the best part about the day had been the skating and the fact that it had made me forget about Matt for a little while. Which, believe it or not, was a relief. Now if only I could keep it up until Valentine's Day passed, everything would be perfect.

CHAPTER 6

Much Ado

"Happy Valentine's Day!" my mom trilled as she popped her head into my room Monday morning to make sure I was awake. I was up, of course, having set my alarm so I'd have time to shower and make my hair look slightly better-than-average before school started. So if I *did* happen to run into Matt at school, at least I'd be ready. After showering and blow-drying and getting dressed in skinny jeans and a cute white sweater with a red heart on it, I hurried down the stairs to see what valentine loot I'd received from my mom.

The table looked really festive with a pink paper tablecloth that was strewn with candy hearts, red napkins, candy-heart-printed paper plates and cups, and a red card and small wrapped red package at each place setting. Even though I was still a little sad about Matt, I had to admit the table looked really pretty.

"Thanks, Mom!" I cried, grabbing the cards I'd bought and distributing one at each place.

Dylan slunk into the room behind me, still in her pj's, rubbing her eyes.

"Dilly? Are you sick?" I asked. Like me, Dylan is an early bird and always dressed and ready by breakfast.

"Aaaah!" she yawned. "I was studying online for the AP English exam with Alvaro Diaz—and then it turned into just texting about stuff and, well . . . I was up really late. I'm soooo tired." She smiled a dreamy smile. Who knew AP English could be so romantic?

"Dylan, that's awful! You'll be exhausted all day at school. You'd better have some protein powder in your smoothie," said my mom. She is a health food nut, though she makes exceptions for birthdays and holidays. She did a U-turn to go back to the blender and doctor up Dylan's smoothie.

Dylan smiled a huge, happy grin. "It wasn't awful! It was great. He asked me to be his valentine!" She giggled. "I mean, Valentine's Day is so dorky, but still. It's nice to be asked, you know?"

I nodded miserably. Yes. Being asked would be nice. Or at least acknowledged in some way, any way. I could feel my mom staring at me, and I refused to meet her eye.

"That's very nice, Dyl," said my mom. "But don't forget it is a silly holiday, and you don't ever want to make it into more than it is."

Dylan rolled her eyes and waved her hand at the kitchen table. "Talk about making more of it than it is!" She laughed.

My mom brought Dylan's protein-improved smoothie over to the table and put it down, then she stood with her hands on her hips. "I do it because I just want you girls to know you're loved here, so you don't have to go seeking it from all corners. You can be picky. There's plenty of love for you right here at home."

"Oh, Mom!" Dylan laughed again. "Come on!"

I thought it was kind of nice, what my mom said, but I also knew it was a little corny.

My mom laughed. She knew too. "I'm serious. Love comes in many forms. It's not all romantic."

"Yes, but the good kind is," said Dylan, and she took a long gulp of her smoothie. "Mmm. Thanks, Mom. I *love* it," she said sarcastically. My mom swatted her playfully on the head with a dish towel.

"Should we open our presents?" I asked.

"Sure!" said my mom.

My dad strolled in, and we all opened our gifts at once. He had bought my mom a pretty red pashmina scarf that she loved. He probably got it from a street vendor in the city, but she was happy. Dylan got red fingerless gloves for texting, a lip balm, and some peanut butter cups in holiday heart shapes. I got a pink ski hat that was soft and supercozy, a lip balm, and some heart-shaped chocolate with nuts. My dad got a red tie from my mom, with little white hearts on it. He took off the tie he had on and swapped it, and it looked really good. Everyone opened their cards, and I was glad I had written a little extra to everyone besides having the preprinted stuff that was already there.

"Thanks, Lex," said Dylan, dropping her card on the table.

"Lovely, sweetheart," said my mom, kissing me on the head after she'd read hers.

"I feel the same way about you!" said my dad, beaming at me. (I had told him I couldn't imagine a better dad in the whole world.)

I beamed back.

My mom stood up again. "Okay, now, let's move along. I have to get to work, and you girls need to eat so you can pay attention in school today."

My heart sank. School. Matt. I chewed on the dry "health bread" toast with peanut butter, gulped down some smoothie, and swallowed the omega-3 capsules my mom always gave me. Then I stood slowly and cleared my plate even slower and then went upstairs to bring up my loot, make my bed, grab my book bag, and go back into the kitchen.

I stole one last glance at my e-mail and texts and then tucked the phone away in my bag. No word from Matt. Nada. Zip. Nothing.

And, despite my mom's advice, that was how I felt too.

I looked up and saw her watching me with a concerned look.

"What?" I said innocently.

She beckoned me into the pantry, and I followed her.

"What? I'm going to be late for school!" I snapped. I knew something annoying was coming, and sometimes I can throw my mom off by invoking school in one way or another.

"I don't care," said my mom, and that was when I knew it was something serious. She spun around and looked me in the eye. "Alexis, you are a smart, ambitious, beautiful girl who makes friends easily and has lots of fabulous skills and interests," she said, staring at me.

"Um . . . so?" I said. Where was this going?

"I saw your face when you checked your texts just now, and I wanted you to know that Sasha mentioned just in passing yesterday that you told her you wanted to skate well to impress a boy at a party."

"But I—" I protested.

"Shh!" commanded my mother. "She didn't mean any harm, she was just joking and saying that from her perspective, whatever it took to motivate people, it was good. Which is fine for her purposes, but it bothered me all night. Alexis, there will be many boys in your life, but only one *you*. I don't want you seeking satisfaction from impressing boys. You will be forever unhappy if that is the case. Young love is fickle and difficult, and your self-worth needs to be measured by your own skills and accomplishments, not by who returns your texts or gives you valentines. Do you understand?"

I nodded.

"Is that a yes?" my mother asked sternly.

"Yes," I said grumpily.

"Matt Taylor is a lovely boy. You know I adore the whole Taylor family. But at your age, you come first. You must remember that. Valentine's Day or no Valentine's Day."

"Fine. I get it," I said. I sounded bratty even to my own ears, but I couldn't think of any other way to be. I was more annoyed that my mom had pinpointed the problem and called me out on it than anything else.

She took a deep breath. "Let's try this again. Alexis first. Boys second, agreed?"

"Agreed," I said.

I clomped upstairs to get a calculator I'd forgotten.

Dylan was doing her hair in the bathroom mirror.

"Did you just get the girl-power speech?" she asked with a big, annoying grin.

I was surprised. I nodded.

Dylan looked back at herself in the mirror. "Mom's right, you know. I've seen some of my friends go batty for boys, and it is a major waste."

"I'm not batty!" I protested. "Why does everyone think I'm batty?"

Dylan looked back at me. "You're not yet, but you're on your way."

"Oh, shush, you!" I said, and I stormed off to school. Batty!

CHAPTER 7

Let's Do Lunch

$\mathcal{M}$onday just kept getting worse. After the morning's love lecture, I pulled the most classic embarrassing moment at school that day: dropping a full lunch tray in the cafeteria.

Talk about mortifying. This surely beats falling down on the ice in front of a group of expert skaters.

What happened was, I was walking away from the lunch line, looking for the Cupcakers' table, when I hit a patch of something slippery on the floor. I skidded, and *boom*! My tray flipped over, and I couldn't right it in time, and the whole contents swooshed onto the floor and made a massive crash!

There was a split second of dead silence, then the usual routine: The whole school clapped, I turned purple with mortification and tried to clean it up, everyone laughed and then went about their business.

And guess what I slipped on?

Ice.

Funny, right?

Not really.

All I could think as I bent to gather the soup bowl (plastic, luckily) and smeared food and spilled water was *At least Matt isn't here right now to see this.* I wanted to freeze the whole room and look around—I hoped that none of his friends in my grade saw me fall. Ugh. I was shaking and practically in tears as my besties arrived at my side.

"Don't worry. I'll help you, Alexis," Emma said comfortingly.

"Here," said Katie, arriving with a pile of napkins, trailed by the maintenance guy with a mop and bucket. The chicken noodle soup had sloshed over my shoe and my pant cuff, and Katie leaned down to blot it.

Mia took stock of what I had selected and ran off to fetch a new tray of food for me.

It was such a comfort to have such good, kind friends.

"We are going to have to get you some balancing

lessons!" someone said. I turned around, and Olivia was standing there with her tray in her hands, smirking. I wanted to hit her tray hard and have all her food go up in her face, but I remembered how Sasha just ignored mean girls, so I did the same and returned to my clean-up attempt.

Emma said all sarcastically, "Oh, Olivia, are you here to help clean up? Or is that a new lunch tray for Alexis? That's so sweet!"

I laughed, and Olivia's face turned red and she walked away.

"Even better than turning the other cheek!" I said to Emma. "Thanks."

"She is too much," said Emma, shaking her head in dismay.

After I apologized to the maintenance man (he waved it off and said, "Happens every day," which I think was him just trying to be nice), Emma and Katie led me over to the table, and Mia followed right behind us with a new tray for me. I sat down and spied a pile of red and pink stuff on the table.

"Hey, what's all this stuff?" I asked.

"Valentines, silly!" Katie laughed. "Duh!"

"Who gave you valentines?" I asked stupidly.

"We gave them to one another. Here are yours," said Mia, tucking a strand of hair behind her ear and pushing three little items over to me.

"But . . . I didn't get you guys anything!" I said, my face turning deep red again. I was so ashamed. I should have realized, that day at the stationery store, of course they were buying things for all of us. I was just so distracted by my Matt drama that I didn't get them anything! My eyes welled with tears.

Emma laughed incredulously. "Oh, Alexis! Don't cry! It's okay. We still love you!"

"I am such a bad friend," I wailed quietly. "And you guys are so good! I am so selfish! And clumsy!"

Katie scooted over and patted me on the back. "Shh. Don't cry. And if you're really upset, you can get us something later, and all the valentine's stuff will be on sale!"

I perked up a little at this. I do love a bargain. I sniffed hard and patted my eyes with a napkin. "This has just been a bad couple of days. I am so sorry."

"Besides the falling down and us not being able to go skating yesterday, is it something else?" Mia asked.

I sighed. I didn't really want to get into the Matt/cupcake thing right now, especially in front of Emma. I felt the most embarrassed about it in front of her. It was all so very humiliating.

Luckily, George Martinez walked up just then. I sat up straight and tried to blink my eyes back to normalcy, but he busted me immediately.

"Sweet tray spill, Becker," he teased. Then he looked more closely at me. "Jeez, you aren't crying about it, are you? I mean, I dropped my tray on chili day! Chili and banana pudding day! It was such a mess, and it got all up my pants, and it was so uncomfortable. . . . Seriously! Have you ever had pudding in your pants?!"

He started mimicking a funny dance, like he was trying to get pudding out of his pants, and everyone started laughing really hard, even me.

"Hey, did you come over here to bring Katie her valentine, George?" asked Mia.

"I don't see any flowers or candy," said Emma, craning her neck like he might be hiding something behind his back. "Maybe you wrote her a poem?" Emma suggested.

Katie blushed a little, but she knew it was all good-natured fun, and besides, she *was* a bit curious to see how George would respond.

"A poem!" George shouted. "How did you ever guess? In fact, I'll recite it right now." He cleared his throat dramatically.

"Roses are red.
Violets are blue.
I like you, Katie.
And your silly arms, too!"

He then took a long exaggerated bow as we all laughed and applauded. "That was fun," George said. "So much so, I almost forgot why I came over here. Oh, yeah! A bunch of us are going to see Liam Carey's new film when it opens this Thursday afternoon, on Teachers' Improvement Day. It's got everything: Epic chase scenes, lots of fighting, and I think there's even a love story, so you girls will like it." George cleared his throat and then said in a high falsetto voice, "I love you, MATT!" And then he deepened his voice to an exaggerated masculine tone and said, "And I love *you*, ALEXIS!"

All the girls giggled, but after the tray drop and Olivia's mean comment and Matt's lack of a response to my valentine, it was all just too much for me to handle. I grabbed my books and rushed out before I started crying again in public. In the hall, I ducked into the girls' bathroom to hide until my next class. It was almost like I needed to just cry and get the tears out. I'd been holding it in for almost two days now. In the stall, I hung my book bag on the hook, grabbed a huge ball of tissues, and wept.

About a minute and a half later, I heard the door open. I knew it would be one of my friends, but I wasn't expecting Emma.

"Lex?" she said.

I sniffed deeply. "Yes?" I croaked.

"Want to come out?" she asked.

"No," I said.

"Ever?" she asked.

"No!" I insisted. "Not ever."

There was a brief silence, and then Emma said, "Want me to take you to the nurse, and she can let you go home?"

Leave school early without being deathly ill? It was unthinkable. I slid the lock and opened the door. I'd rather die than go home sick, especially if I wasn't! Emma sure knew how to get me.

I sighed heavily. "I am such a loser," I said, leaning against the side of the stall.

Emma laughed. "You are insane. You're not a loser! Seriously? You're the biggest winner of us all! You get the best grades, you're involved in running a business and your business leaders extracurriculars, and you're a great singer and dancer . . ."

"But I'm a terrible ice-skater. And no one loves me," I said, moping.

"Alexis Becker. You've got to come clean with me. I'm your oldest friend in the world. Is there something going on that I should know about?" Emma asked sternly.

I hesitated.

"Is this about Matt?" she asked gently.

I finally broke down and told Emma all about the valentine cupcake I had given Matt and how I had never heard from him about it. Unsurprisingly, Emma was furious.

"I know he isn't the mushy type, but to not even say thank you . . . that's just so rude and so wrong," she said. "Just wait until I see him tonight!"

"Noooo! Emma, please! That will only make me feel worse," I cried. "Please, don't say a word— promise me!" I begged. "That's why I didn't say anything to begin with!"

Reluctantly, she agreed, but she huffed, "Okay, but I still think it's rude. And honestly, it's pretty out of character. I just can't believe he wouldn't even acknowledge it. Even if he only liked you as a friend. It's just weird."

"Do you think I just totally scared him off?" I asked, wincing.

Emma thought for a minute. "No. Definitely not. Boys like it when girls like them, you know. And it's not like you're some weird nerd. . . ."

"Thanks. Thanks a lot," I said, and we giggled, which felt good.

Emma corrected herself. "You're a total babe, and he'd be lucky to have someone as great as you as his valentine!"

Turning red again, I said something else that was really bothering me. "Do you think George or any of Matt's friends in our grade will tell Matt about my embarrassing fall?"

Emma thought for a second. "I don't think George will—it's not as good of a story as him getting pudding out of his own pants!"

"Oh, thank goodness!" I sighed with relief. "That would have been the icing on the cake."

"Or the cupcake!" said Emma, and then we both giggled. Emma gave me a big hug. "That's better," she said. "Don't worry about stupid boys, anyway. We have lots of fun coming up this week. The new Liam Carey movie on Thursday, the Family Skating Party on Friday . . . you valentine's shopping the bargain basement sale for us!"

I put my head in my hands. "I am so mortified about that."

"Oh, Lex, I'm just kiddin' ya!" said Emma. "Come on. Let's go, valentine!"

I grabbed my book bag and we exited the bathroom.

"By the way," said Emma with a sly grin, "George said to tell you that Matt is going to the movies on Thursday. I'm just saying!" She put her hands in the air, palms out, like *Don't shoot the messenger!*

"Well, then I'm not going," I declared.

"Hey, you can't lead your life like that," Emma scolded. "Stop worrying about embarrassment and just get on with your life. Have fun. Seriously. Who cares what Matt—or anyone—thinks? Where's the bold, brassy future business leader who I know and love?"

"In hiding," I said. I saw her point, but I still wasn't sure.

"You have all these friends who love you, and a great family, and that is pretty awesome," she said as we reached her classroom door.

"You sound like my mom," I whined.

Emma wheeled around to face me. "Then that's a compliment, 'cause your mom is one smart cupcake!" she said with a grin, and she strode into her class.

I went to my next class like a tentative baby

chick, hoping no one would bring up the tray drop or anything else for the rest of the day. Or my life.

I wasn't ready to commit to the movie or the skating party at this point. Bargain valentines shopping for my besties, *maybe*.

CHAPTER 8

Time Out

*T*hat night, after I finished my homework, I spent some time on YouTube, toggling back and forth between Olympic gold medal skating programs and "How to Skate" videos. Both were discouraging. The Olympians looked so much like ballroom-dancing stars that I had to keep reminding myself that they were doing everything while simultaneously gliding on a sharp blades across hard, slippery ice at twenty miles an hour! It was pretty incredible when I looked at it that way. I couldn't imagine the endless hours Sasha had spent at an ice rink perfecting her skills. I didn't have that kind of time before Friday's party.

It must've been ESP, because while I was doing that, Katie sent a group chat to say the Cupcake

Club had been hired by the PTA to bake ten dozen Chinese-themed cupcakes for the bake sale at the skating party on Friday! Now that was the kind of news I liked, because there's nothing I find more fun than making money with my friends.

Since I was already online, I volunteered to google around and come up with a couple of possible Chinese cupcake ideas. I had two criteria: the ingredients couldn't be too expensive, because the PTA had set a small budget for the job, and the design and assembly couldn't be too fussy, or it would take us too long to make them. Sometimes when we have an elaborate job or a huge order, we will do it over a couple of days, but I honestly think our cupcakes taste best when they are superfresh: made, decorated, and eaten all in one day.

When I went on Pinterest to look for Chinese cupcake ideas, what I found was gorgeous, but waaaaay too complicated for us. They looked like something from one of those *Cake Boss* shows we all loved so much. We'd need scaffolding and blowtorches and stuff to make some of those ideas.

I thought of doing a clear or white glaze across a white cupcake, so that it might look like skating "ice" (get it? "Icing"?!), but the more I thought about it, the more I thought people wouldn't get the joke and also—worse—wouldn't think the cupcakes tasted any good. Taste had to come first.

Then I stumbled upon the perfect idea: panda cupcakes! Pandas are a big thing in China, right? So I started searching all the panda cupcake images I could find (they are so cute—try it sometime!) and finally found one that looked simple enough. We'd only need plain cake (maybe do five dozen yellow cake and five dozen chocolate cake), plain white or silver foil wrappers, white frosting, tubes of brown frosting for piping (maybe a gel, if it looked opaque enough), and brown M&Ms for ears. They'd be easy to make—just frost the cake in white, pipe on the facial features in dark brown, and pop in two M&M's for ears. Done!

I attached a photo to an e-mail and sent it to the others, and within minutes everyone had agreed it was perfect. I volunteered to go buy the supplies, since I was heading to the mall the next day, anyway—for some, ahem, bargain valentines—and everyone agreed.

I closed down my computer for the night with a feeling of deep satisfaction that held my mortification about Matt and the tray drop, as well as my anxiety about skating, at bay for the rest of the night.

I managed to avoid thinking about Matt the whole next day at school, which was a relief to know I could do that. For lunch, I had Mia bring me a sandwich that I could eat in the library to avoid another spill in the cafeteria, and I read some articles about the physics of balancing on ice-skates. It was kind of fun, I had to admit.

After school, I rode my bike to the mall and texted my mom to pick me up after. I'd just put my bike on the rack. I expected I'd have some big packages, and anyway, I am not crazy about riding my bike after dark alone, even though I have a helmet, reflectors, and two flashing lights on it. (Dylan calls me a nerd on wheels when she sees me in full safety gear, but I just don't care. *Better dork than dead,* I always tell her.)

At the mall, I locked my bike and headed in. My first stop was the stationery store, and I hit the jackpot! There was a whole wall of valentine stuff, and I almost didn't know where to begin. I had set a budget of twenty-five dollars for everything, and I was in luck. Everything was 75 percent off for clearance. First, I got each friend a sweet card for about a dollar each. Then I found these adorable little white baskets filled with assorted red candy, topped with a red ribbon that had tiny white polka dots all over it. So sweet. They were marked down from fifteen dollars to just five dollars each! I was thrilled. I made a mental note to tell the others that next year we are celebrating Valentine's Day on the sixteenth of February. We'd be crazy not to!

I was in heaven as I paid the clerk (same lady as the other day!), and then I headed to Baker's Hollow on the other side of the food court. As I crossed through, I could have sworn I saw someone who looked just like Matt standing at the Panda Gardens counter, but I quickly looked away as my stomach clenched in fear. I tried to steal another glance, but I was at a bad angle, and he might be able to catch me looking if I did. So instead I kept my head high and continued on, my heart pounding and my butterflies fluttering even more than usual.

Breathless, I reached Baker's Hollow and barreled inside. The sweet old lady at the counter gave me a funny look and said, "Everything all right, dear?" I huffed and puffed and tried to calm myself down. I gulped. My heart was beating so fast!

"Yes." I gasped. "I'm fine. Sorry. Just ran here . . ."

She giggled kindly. "Well, we're always glad to hear our customers run to our store! Now just let me know if you need anything."

I thanked her and grabbed a basket. My list was short and clear. A pound and a half of dark brown M&M's (generic brand, of course) from the dispensers. Ten tubes of brown decorating frosting with a fine-point tip. Plain cupcake papers. I considered buying some edible googly eyes that were really cute and would save us some time and labor, but when I looked at the price, I gasped aloud. They were $19.99 a pound! No can do, googlies!

I went to pay the lady, and as I looked over her shoulder and out the plate-glass window, I saw him again. Definitely Matt. Ugh! I could feel my face turning bright red, and I tried to maneuver myself behind a display of bread makers, so I couldn't be seen from outside.

"Sweetie? Are you not finished shopping?" called the lady.

"Oh, sorry! Just remembered one other thing!" I buried myself deep in the store for a moment, and then I returned to the register, frantically scanning the "sidewalk" outside the store. He was gone. The coast was clear. I breathed a large sigh of relief.

"Phew," I said. Accidentally out loud. Oops.

The lady gave me a strange look and told me my total. I could feel her still looking at me closely as I counted out my change, and finally, she leaned across the counter and put her hand on mine and said in the kindest voice, "Listen, dear, if there's someone out there who is bothering you, please feel welcome to stay in the store while I call security. Is it a bully from school?"

I looked up, confused for a moment, and then I laughed. Hardly. In fact, the opposite! Now it was the lady's turn to look confused.

"Thank you so much," I said. "That is so nice of you. I'm just . . ." I lowered my voice and decided she seemed like the type who could handle the truth. "I gave a boy a valentine and he never acknowledged it. And I just saw him out there"— I shrugged—"so, you know . . . I'm avoiding him!" I stage-whispered.

The saleslady stage-whispered back conspiratorially, "You know, I had the same thing happen when I was young. Maybe a bit older than you, but still. I gave a boy a valentine, and he didn't reciprocate. Turned out it was because he had bought something for me that seemed shabby in comparison, and he didn't know what to do. He wanted to get me something better, but he couldn't afford it, so he was stuck. So sweet."

"Oh, that's so cute!" I said. "So what happened?"

"I married him!" She laughed.

Now it was my turn to laugh. "Wow! That story sure has a happy ending!"

She smiled. "I know. All I'm saying is, there's often more than meets the eye. Most boys are good people, so don't read too much into it. I should know, because I ended up having four boys of my own!"

"Lucky you," I said.

She nodded and handed me my bag. "Come on back and let me know what happens, okay? My name's Sadie."

"I'm Alexis. I hope my ending is as happy as yours!"

"Me too. Good luck, now, and thanks for shopping with us."

"Bye!"

On my way out of the store I looked left and right, and the coast was clear. He'd surely left by now.

I looked at my watch. Ten minutes till my mom was due. I'd have just enough time to pop into the bookstore and see if they had *Figure Skating for Dummies*. I needed all the help I could get!

I hitched the two bags up over my shoulder, satchel style, and trooped back across the food court to the bookstore on the far side. Just in case, I kept my eyes locked straight ahead, looking neither left nor right. If Matt was there, I'd never know, and I'd spare him the horror of having to speak to me.

But as I passed the seating area, I suddenly heard his voice.

"Alexis!" he called.

I turned and blushed simultaneously. He was sitting alone, eating a plate of fried rice.

"Hey," I said, playing it cool.

"Hey!" he said, smiling, but it was kind of tentative, like now that he'd called out to me, he wasn't sure what to say. I think he was surprised by my coolness, too.

"Um, anything up?" I asked casually.

I saw his face fall a little. Then he started playing it cool too. "Oh. Nah, just . . . grabbing a quick bite, then riding back to school for a game." He shrugged. There was an awkward silence. He looked like he was waiting for me to say something, but I wasn't sure what he expected. Like, should I apologize for giving him a valentine? Whatever. I wasn't about to do that—not here, anyway. Not now.

"So . . ." I shrugged. "I guess I'd better get going."

"Yeah. Right. Okay. Bye," he said, all business-like, like he was done with me. Like he regretted even calling out to me.

"See ya," I said, turning on my heel.

"Yeah," he said. I could almost hear the "whatever" at the end, even though he didn't say it out loud.

Fine, I thought. *That's just fine.* I trudged away with my bags, knowing he wasn't watching me go, which was a relief in a weird way.

So this is how it ends, I thought. In a mall. Me walking away. Him just sitting there. The whole thing spoiled by a dumb holiday and some maybe overly optimistic gift. Fine, then. I'm done with him. If he can't even have the common decency to thank me, or deal with the weirdness head-on, then he's not the one for me. I wouldn't want to be with someone who had such bad manners, anyway.

I reached the bookstore, yanked the door open a little harder than necessary, and located the skating book in the sports section. I flipped through it and decided it wasn't worth the money. Who could learn skating from a dumb old book, anyway. And who cared if I could skate well or not? I'd just go to the party to drop off the cupcakes on Friday, and then I'd head out. That's all.

It was time to go meet my mom. I peeked out toward the food court, and just as I expected, Matt was gone. *Good riddance,* I thought. I won't have to see him for a while.

Then my brain started working and my memory kicked in like a ton of bricks.

I'd be seeing him tomorrow at the new Liam Carey movie.

If I went, that is.

CHAPTER 9

BFF

After the mall, I put Matt right out of my mind. I went home, did my homework, and organized the valentines and gifts for my friends. I showered, organized my schoolwork, tweaked my presentation for the FBLA summit, laid out my outfit for the next day, and got into bed with a good book. I simply refused to think about him.

The next morning I woke up kind of sad, but I shook it off. I told myself I was over Matt and that was that. From now on, I was all about my family, my friends, and my work, in that order. It was kind of a relief to be done with him and all that "mushy stuff," as Emma put it. I felt sharp and focused and independent. It was good. Anytime he popped into my head, I pushed him out. Mind over matter! No problem! Alexis first—boys second!

That day, I brought the valentine stuff to school, and at lunchtime in the cafeteria, we all met up at our usual corner table, where I presented the things to my friends.

"Ta-da!" I cried. "Better late than never!"

"Thanks, Alexis!' said Katie.

"It's a shockingly good feeling to have been more organized than you for once," Emma said with a laugh. "When was the last time we beat Alexis to *any*thing?"

They all had a good chuckle over that one.

A little too good, if you ask me.

"All right, all right, it wasn't *that* funny," I fake-fumed. "Break it up."

They opened their cards and oohed and aahed over the candy baskets.

"They are just too cute!" said Mia. "*LOVE* the ribbons. Thank you *SO* much, Alexis!" She wound the ribbon over her hand in a loop and tucked it in her pocket.

"*Thank you!* I think I saw these somewhere. Did you get them at the stationery store at the mall?" Katie asked, wrinkling her brow.

"Uh-huh. Seventy-five percent off!" I bragged.

"Nothing but the best for your friends. Thanks, old buddy, old pal!" joked Mia.

Emma looked at the baskets as though she was trying to remember something. "I know I've seen one of these before somewhere. It wasn't at the stationery store. I just can't think of where it was." She tapped her lip for a minute, then she shrugged and said, "Oh well. I'm eating some candy right now! Thanks, Lex!"

"Before your lunch?" I said disapprovingly, joking. "That is just not healthy."

Emma laughed and then shrugged. "YOLO! You know—you only live once!

"Sounds good!" said Katie, diving into hers.

I had to sit back and smile. They were enjoying the stuff I gave them. Maybe Valentine's Day could be fun after all!

It wasn't until that afternoon that I began to actually panic about Matt. We were at Katie's to bake the cupcakes for Friday, knowing we wouldn't have time to bake them tomorrow. Things were moving along quickly, since Katie has two ovens, and since she is an only child, so there are absolutely no distractions, like brothers at the Taylors' house.

Toward the end of our session, as rows of future

plump pandas sat cooling on racks, Mia asked, "Are you guys going to go home before the movie tomorrow or straight to the theater?"

Emma answered, "My dad is going to pop over from work, because he has to bring Jake to us to watch him. He's going to give me and Matt a lift to the movies from school, since Jake can't ride that far on a bike. He can take any of you, if you'd like."

"Great! I'd love it!" agreed Mia.

"Me too, thanks," said Katie.

I didn't say anything, but I felt a pit in my stomach. So this was how it was going to be from now on. All my besties, riding to the movies together with my former crush. And me, riding solo. Biking, actually. Wow.

"Lex? Ride?" Emma asked absentmindedly, like she knew I would be in.

"Uh, actually, no. But thanks. You guys go on, and I'll meet you there."

They all turned and stared at me.

"Why?" Mia asked incredulously.

I shrugged. "Oh, it's a lot of people for the minivan. . . ."

"It seats eight," said Katie. "We're only at six."

There was a brief silence, then Emma said quietly, "Is this about Matt?"

"No!" I said a little too forcefully. "No, no," I added more casually. "I just ... have some stuff, so I'll see you there." I smiled, all fake-cherry. "Seriously. No prob."

Emma continued to look hard at me, then she shrugged and raised an eyebrow at the others, and they all looked away. Now I was embarrassed and kind of mad, because I knew that meant they'd all be discussing me later.

See, this is why it's not a good idea to have a crush on your best friend's brother. 'Cause when it's over, there's no way to get away.

In fact, maybe liking boys is just more trouble than it's worth. It certainly seems to mess up your friendships while you're at it.

I focused on my task of setting the cooled cakes in their travel containers, so we could seal them up for the night. They'd have to be ready to decorate on Friday, and then we'd tote them over to the skating party, after which point I would turn on my heel and head home. Maybe I'd rent a movie. Nothing romantic. Not at all.

Our baking session ended, and we were all getting ready to leave. Mia's mom was picking her up, and she offered to drive me and Emma home, but we both refused politely. It wasn't that far to walk, and the brisk air would feel good after the warm, sweet-smelling kitchen.

"I'll go with you, Lex," said Emma.

It sounded more like a command than an offer, so I said, "Fine."

We all said good-bye, and Emma and I set out. Even though at first I enjoyed the chilly air, it started to get a little too cold for us, and we both began to move more quickly. The ice crunched under us.

"Alexis," Emma said after almost a block of silence, "you are my best friend, and I think it's really mean you're letting your Matt drama get in the way of our friendship."

I'd known it would be coming. I just didn't realize she'd take the aggressive tack right out of the gate. It made me feel defensive. I breathed out a long puff of air and watched the smokelike vapor hang in front of me. I considered how to reply.

Finally, I said, "I don't want to be in a fight with you, Emma. I just . . . I'm not even sure I want to go tomorrow. It's just still too raw. Did you know I saw him at the mall last night?" I asked, wincing at the memory.

She turned and looked at me. "No. He didn't mention it."

I nodded. "Well, it was really, really awkward.

He almost acted like he was . . . mad at me or hurt or something, which is really weird. I mean, obviously I didn't give him a valentine to be *mean*! And I'm actually kind of mad at *him* right now. Besides being embarrassed, that is. So, I am sure it will get better one day, but right now I just don't want to be around him. I'll do my best to figure out how to be around you without that getting in the way, though. Does that make sense?"

Emma nodded. She was a rational person. I mean, she *is* my best friend after all. But then she said, "Okay. But if you don't come to the movie with us tomorrow like we've all planned, then you're not my best friend anymore. And I'm only kind of joking when I say that. It's going to be so much fun! I really wish you'd reconsider."

The rest of our walk was a little awkward, to say the least. And by the time I got home, all I could think was, *Great. Now I've got the whole Taylor family against me.*

At dinner, my mom tipped her head at an angle and studied me. I knew I was being mopey, but I didn't have the energy to be otherwise.

"Honey, you love salmon teriyaki," said my mom. "Eat up!"

I pushed a piece of broccoli around on my plate and sighed.

"Still having a tough time of it?" asked my mom. She looked at my dad, and he raised his eyebrows. Right then, I knew they'd been discussing me, which is always annoying.

"About what?" I asked. I wasn't going to give them an inch, those traitors! Talking about me behind my back!

"What's up, people?" said Dylan, clueing in to the conversation. "I smell drama."

"Gosh, what is this, family therapy?" I huffed.

"It can be if you want it to," said my mom.

"No, *thanks!*" I said vehemently. I stabbed a piece of salmon and forced myself to eat it to show I was fine, even though I wasn't very hungry.

"Middle school troubles?" said Dylan. "Those were the days. I had it so easy. Who knew at the time?"

"All right, Dilly, enough," my dad said, laughing a little.

"Seriously, Alexis. What's the deal? Tell your big sister. Maybe I can help. Remember, I've seen it all."

I hesitated for a second, then figured, *What the heck?*

95

I explained about Matt and the cupcake. Then I told them about the mall and Emma.

"Oh, sweetheart. She's just hurt and maybe a little jealous," said my mom. "You two have been such good friends for so long!"

"Well, I think it's mean and immature," Dylan said fiercely.

"Thanks," I said.

"But more to the point, *why oh why* didn't you consult me first before giving Matt a valentine?" Dylan moaned.

I shrugged. "I didn't think of it. It was just . . . impulsive!" I said.

Dylan stared at me. "Never. Be. Impulsive. When. It. Comes. To. Boys. Get it?"

I gulped. "Okay," I agreed meekly.

"Excellent advice!" my father said, nodding vigorously. "I couldn't agree with you more, my dear."

My mom was nodding too, so I guess we had a consensus.

"Let's move on," said Dylan. "It was a bold move, and I commend you for that." She flipped her hair. "We will continue with this conversation after dinner in the privacy of my own room, where we will come up with our plan of action."

Then she gave me a meaningful glare.

"Right!" I agreed.

"Nothing bold! Nothing impulsive!" my dad added.

"Right," agreed Dylan. And she winked at me.

Right, I thought. *Here we go!*

CHAPTER 10

New You

"Of course you're going. You *have* to go. And you have to look *fabulous*," commanded Dylan. "Make him see what he's missing! And when you see him, give him a big smile, but then ignore him."

"Wait. I'm confused," I said. She'd almost had me up until then, but that part made no sense. "Smile . . . then ignore him? I don't get it."

"Exactly!" Dylan cheered. "You'll be intriguing . . . mysterious . . . exciting! He won't know what you'll do next."

"Oh. Okaaaay?" I wasn't too sure.

"Now," she continued, "if you *do* catch his eye, try to look mysterious."

I was completely baffled. "What does *mysterious* even look like?"

"Like this," said Dylan. She gave her head a toss, lowered her chin, and let the front lock of her long hair drop over one eye. She looked up and kind of widened her eyes, then she looked down and away. It was totally weird and phony looking, like a girl villain from a cartoon or something.

"Um, yeah. That is totally not me, so I don't think I'll be doing it." I almost shuddered at the idea.

"Well, practice, anyway. A little mystery goes a long way. Remember that," Dylan said. "Now, let's talk about your outfit. We'll lay it out tonight. I'm thinking jewel tones. Powerful. Bright. Confident. Don't you think?"

"Sounds good," I said. I was curious to see what kind of outfit Dylan put together for me, even if I didn't go to the movies in the end. Dylan started flipping briskly through the hangers in her closet. The girl *does* enjoy a good makeover.

"Aha!" she said. She pulled out a vintage leopard-skin patterned dress. "This, for sure! Me-*ow*!" She made her hand into a claw and pretended to scratch the air with it.

But I was already shaking my head. "Seriously, Dyl? To wear to the movies? In the afternoon?"

"Oh, right. I was getting a little carried away."

Push, push, push—the hangers squeaked along the metal pole in rapid succession.

"Okay, now *here* we go. *That's* what I'm talkin' about!" Dylan pulled a black leather biker jacket from the rod and held it toward me on its hanger. "Go on. Put it on. This thing was made for tomorrow."

"Where did you even get this?" I laughed. "Mom and Dad would never let me go out in this." But I shrugged it on anyway and turned to look in the mirror.

"I got it in a vintage store in the city. Killer, right?" she said.

"Yeah. More like, I look like a killer. I don't think so," I said, taking it off and handing it back to her. "Sorry."

Dylan pursed her lips. "You are not making this easy. Okay. Think, Dylan, think," she scolded herself. She stood in front of the closet and heaved a big thoughtful sigh. Then, after a minute, she continued thinking out loud, talking to herself.

"Okay. We want her to look fantastic. Her best color. But casual. Superperfect, but looking like she hasn't tried. Like 'This old thing?' Okay."

She reached up on her shelf and brought down

one of her prized possession: a beautiful deep emerald-green cashmere turtleneck sweater given to her by her godmother. It was thick and fuzzy, folded perfectly, still with the dry-cleaning tissue wrapped around it. Reverently, she held it out to me. The way it caught the light, it almost seemed to glow.

I put up my palms in protest. "Oh, Dylan. I couldn't. That is so nice. Seriously. Thanks."

Dylan nodded. "I know," she whispered. "But you really need to wear this. Please. Take it."

"Thank you," I whispered back. "I promise I'll take good care of it. *If* I go."

"Put it on," Dylan commanded in a normal voice.

Quickly, I whipped off my shirt and pulled the sweater on over my head. It felt wonderful against my skin, like the softest baby blanket in the world. Popping my head out of the top, I blinked and pushed my hair out of my eyes. Dylan was there to primp.

"Here, fold the turtleneck down, I think. And then fluff your hair like so . . ." She tweaked the waistline and where it sat, and then she gave a gentle tug to align everything. Then Dylan nodded happily. "Yes!" she shouted. "Just look!"

I turned around and looked in her full-length mirror. I couldn't believe how nice I looked.

I gasped. "It's fantastic! It's . . . it's magical! It's so pretty, I could cry!"

"It's ridiculous how good that sweater looks. Like it was made for you. Emerald green is definitely your color," Dylan said.

I turned back, drew closer to the mirror, and I had to admit she was right. The emerald green complimented my pale skin perfectly, made my eyes sparkle, and my red hair glow. What's more, it fit me perfectly, and boy, did it feel wonderful on. She was right. I had to wear it.

"Um, okay. You're right. I'll wear it. But with what?"

"Something casual. Something that makes the sweater look like, 'This old thing?' What do you have for pants? Cords, maybe?"

"Oh! I have those new cream cords? I was kind of saving them, but—"

"Perfect! Go get them. And you can wear them with those brown leather boots Grandma got me for Christmas."

I dashed into my room and rummaged to the bottom of my pants drawer and found the cream cords I'd gotten at Big Blue when my grandmother took me and Dylan shopping for the January sales. They were also soft and cozy. It would be a fitting way to break them in. I threw them on, fixed the sweater's hemline, and popped back into Dylan's room.

"Here are the boots," said Dylan.

"All your favorite things, Dilly? Are you sure?"

"Yes. You need to come out with all guns blazing!"

The boots were a teeny-weeny bit too small (my feet are bigger than hers, and I'm almost taller than Dylan already), but she said I could wear a thin sock and still rock them, so I couldn't refuse. The outfit looked awesome—more like someone in their twenties would wear than someone in middle school.

I grinned at Dylan, but she was looking at me appraisingly again. "The hair," she said.

I put my hand to my head. "What?"

"We'll need to fix it. What time's the movie tomorrow?"

"Four o'clock."

She nodded, "Yup. Let's do it. Come home straight from school. Quick shower, then I'll blow it out and make it all smooth and wavy the way you like it."

"Really? Like, don't you have four million other things to do?"

She smiled. "I'm meeting Alvaro at the café when his band practice is over! At five!"

I smiled. "Love has made you very generous," I said.

She shrugged. "I was always generous. I just found you annoying, so I rarely gave you anything."

"Way to burst my bubble, Dyl." I laughed. "Thanks a lot."

"Kid-ding!" she singsonged.

"I'm going to go take this all off. Tomorrow, I'll change into it when I get home, after you do my hair! Then at the movies—"

"Wait, so you're definitely going?" asked Dylan. "I wasn't sure."

"What? Oh. Yeah. I think I'd better, don't you? I mean, why waste this outfit?" I said, and off I went to change.

The next day at school, Emma sidled up to me in the hall. "You're coming, right?" I think it had turned into a test of friendship or something for her.

I nodded. "Yup. All set!"

"Great!" She brightened. She must've been

thinking I'd say no. "Then I have good news. You can come with us. Matt's going over to George's after school, so we have plenty of room in the car." She grinned at me. "Okay?"

"Oh, that's so nice. Thanks. But I have to go home first, and, uh . . . I have just one thing to do. So that's okay. I can just ride my bike." Ugh. I winced, picturing myself riding my bike along the dirty streets in my cream pants.

Luckily, Emma was having none of it. "Okay, then we'll pick you up at three thirty at your house. Okay?"

"Okay," I agreed. "See you then."

After school, I dashed home, hopped in the shower, and when I came out, Dylan had arrived. I sat on a stool in front of her full-length mirror, and she got to work, spritzing and pinning and sometimes pulling. (I didn't dare yelp for fear she'd quit.) Dylan is really quite handy with beauty stuff. The girl really knows her way around a blow-dryer. My hair began to cooperate, and soon it looked beautiful—bouncing and behaving and shiny. Much fancier than I ever usually wear it.

"Almost done!" Dylan cautioned as I tried to touch a long, loopy curl.

"Sorry," I muttered.

Soon, she turned off the dryer. "Perfect!" she exclaimed, surveying her handiwork as she walked around me, spraying a toxic cloud of hairspray. "And now for makeup."

"Uh, this morning Mom told me we need to use a really light hand if I do makeup...."

"Of course!" said Dylan. "You don't need to tell me! I've got it under control. A teeny, tiny dab of brown mascara. And just the *slightest* hint of lip gloss."

I looked at my watch: 3:25. "They'll be here in five minutes. Should I get dressed now?"

Dylan made sweeping motions toward my room with her hand, so I scampered off and pulled on the miracle outfit. When I went back across the hall, Dylan shook her head from side to side, smiling in marvel. "Just right!" she said. "Love the full effect with the hair. Now sit!" she barked, so I did.

She did as she promised and only used a tiny bit of makeup. When the car horn sounded outside— *toot, toot*—she pressed a pair of earrings into my hand—gold knotted studs—and the lip gloss. I gave her a huge hug. "Thanks, Dylan! You're the best big sister ever!" Then I ran downstairs, jabbing the studs into my ears, and then swiping the lip gloss across my mouth. I pulled on my coat and hurried out to the driveway, where everyone was waiting in the Taylors' minivan.

The door whooshed open, and I climbed aboard. Mr. Taylor called out a greeting, and we were on our way.

"Whoa!" cried Mia. "Lookin' good!"

I smiled, feeling shy. "Thanks."

"You look really pretty, Alexis," agreed Katie.

Emma leaned close to my ear and whispered, "If he doesn't see what he's missing today, Matt's an idiot, even if he is my brother."

"Thanks. That means a lot to me to hear you say it," I said. It really did.

Just then Jake popped up from the back row. "Alexis! Are you going to a party? Why are you all dressed up?" Everyone laughed as Emma scolded him back into his seat and buckled his seat belt.

"I can't believe your folks are letting him see this movie," I whispered to Emma.

She nodded. "It's PG. We'll just distract him if there's a really bad part," she answered in a low voice.

I turned to face forward, took a deep breath, and steeled myself as we pulled up in front of the mall.

It was Go Time!

CHAPTER 11

Showtime

Jake dragged us straight to the concession stand. My stomach was in knots so maybe eating something would help. But it had to be just plain popcorn and water, so nothing happened to the sweater.

Jake went first. "I'll have a huge tub of popcorn with butter, a Buncha Crunch, a large Coke . . ."

"Hey, slow down, mister!" Emma said in exasperation. "I'm not spending twenty-five bucks on snacks for you to have you spill it anyway. You're getting a small soda and a small popcorn, like you always do."

Jake pouted.

I bent down and whispered. "Hey, it was worth a try."

He rolled his eyes and nodded. He knew when

he was defeated. Then he spied someone over my shoulder. "Matt! Over here!"

Ugh. My stomach clenched. I didn't even want to turn around, but it would be too weird not to. I kind of half turned, and as I caught sight of Matt, and he caught sight of me, his jaw actually dropped. I swear! And he stopped in his tracks for a minute. Then a huge grin spread across his face, and he started walking toward us.

"Alexis?" he said, like he wasn't sure it was me.

I scrambled to think of Dylan's advice. I nodded, and kind of half smiled, then looked away and down. Then I fluttered my eyelashes a little. I think that was part of it, right? I tried to droop my hair onto my forehead, but it was sprayed firmly into place, so I wound up kind of squinting.

Matt reached my side. "You look so nice, Alexis. Hey . . . do you have something in your eye?" He looked at me in concern.

"Uh, no . . . I . . ." I cleared my throat. "No. I'm fine. Thanks." So much for mysterious! Clearly, he was happy to see me, or something, but now I was at a loss. I looked away.

"Did Dad give you guys money for me?" asked Matt.

Emma appeared and handed him ten bucks and

a ticket. "Soo . . . doesn't Alexis look pretty?" she sang out with an evil grin.

I turned dark red, and so did Matt. "Um, yeah. Really pretty," he agreed nervously. Then he quickly stepped to the counter to order his candy.

"Thanks a lot!" I hissed at Emma. "I am so out of here!"

"Oh, stop. I'm just having a little fun!" she whispered. Then she called, "Matt! We're going to get seats!"

"Okay," he called, without really turning around.

"You see? He won't even look at me!" I cried when we were out of earshot and headed into the darkened theater.

Emma laughed. "It's not that he *won't*, you dope! It's that he *can't*! You're like the sun, all dazzling in your emerald green and your gorgeous shiny hair! He can't look at you or he'll start grinning like an idiot! Come on. Cut the guy some slack. It's a good thing!" She elbowed me.

Now I think it was my turn for my jaw to drop. "Seriously? Do you really think that?"

"I don't think it, I know it. Trust me."

"Humph," I said. The butterflies in my stomach starting doing a happy nervous dance, which is better than just a scared nervous dance. I pictured butterflies fluttering around in my stomach, all colorful and synchronized, like Olivia's skating team. It made me giggle.

Walking down the aisle, we heard Mia and Katie calling us over. Jake went first, to sit next to his beloved Mia, then me, then Emma. George and the boys filed in and sat right behind us as the trailers started. The lights were still pretty bright, so everyone was whispering and chatting over the row. Everyone but me and Matt, that is.

Mia was asking Jake if he was nervous about the scary parts of the movie, and he said no, because he'd brought his Emma Bear. He reached down inside his backpack and pulled out the beloved bear he'd gotten when he had his tonsils out. (He'd named it after Emma because she looked after him at the hospital.)

"Oh, I love her pretty new ribbon! It's just like the one—" Mia began.

Suddenly, Matt called out, kind of angry, "Hey! Jake! Where'd you get that ribbon?"

Jake quickly grabbed the bear from Mia and tried to shove it back into his knapsack. Matt practically jumped over the seat and wrenched the bear out of Jake's hand. What was going on? I turned to look at Matt, and he was examining the ribbon.

It was red, with tiny white polka dots. It must've come from the candy I gave Emma. Except hadn't she thrown that away at school? I was confused. Was it Mia's? I knew she had saved hers.

"Where did you get this ribbon, Jake?" repeated Matt.

"I . . . It was on the candy! I—I was still a little hungry after I ate the cupcake on your desk, and I saw the candy in the hall, so . . ."

"Wait, the cupcake on *Matt's* desk?" I cried.

Jake nodded and sank down in his seat, folding his arms across his chest and sulking. "I was hungry, and everyone was being mean to me and saying I can't have a cupcake, so I ate that one because no one would know."

"That cupcake was for Matt! It was his valentine!" I yelped. "I worked really hard decorating that!"

"It was really pretty, Alexis," Jake said, patting my arm with his chubby little hand.

I had to laugh in shock, thinking of all the time I'd wasted worrying about what Matt thought about one lousy little cupcake. One lousy little cupcake that Jake had wolfed down before Matt even knew it was there! The whole thing was ridiculous! What a complete waste of time and energy!

But Matt was angry, and I couldn't figure out why.

"Jake! The candy in the hall was on Alexis's tablet because it was for Alexis!" Matt was practically shouting.

Jake shrugged. "I didn't know. No one was there, so it looked like I could just have it." He turned to face the movie screen and acted like he was totally engrossed.

"Why didn't you tell us?" I asked.

"Nobody asked!" said Jake.

"Oh, for goodness's sake!" I practically shouted.

"Shh!" shushed someone from the balcony.

Matt began to whisper. "You left me a cupcake?"

I grinned and nodded. "Yeah, I guess it was kind of lame, but . . ."

"It was yummy! And it had icing and hearts, too!" said Jake.

"Shh!" Matt said to Jake. Then he turned back to me. "Thanks. I wish I saw it."

I shrugged. "You left me candy?"

Now it was Matt's turn to shrug. "It was just in a little white basket, with a ribbon. There wasn't much candy but I thought it was kind of pretty, so . . ."

"I know! I bought the same thing for the other Cupcakers. On sale, though," I added. I couldn't help realizing he'd bought it for *me* at full price. Wow. That was pretty major. "It was really pretty, so thanks!"

"It *was* pretty. That's why I kept the ribbon!" Jake piped.

"Shh!" I said.

Matt and I looked at each other. "Thanks," we both said at the same time. Then we both laughed.

"That was why I was upset when I saw you at the mall. . . . I thought you got the candy and didn't say anything," said Matt. "I was mortified."

"Me too! I was so mad and embarrassed when you didn't say anything about the cupcake." I laughed. What a silly, stupid waste of time!

The trailers ended and the movie began. The theater grew even darker.

I felt a hand pat my shoulder, and I knew it wasn't Jake. I put my hand on top of Matt's hand for a second and then patted him back. Swoon!

Then Matt leaned down and whispered, "Next time, I'll get you flowers. I don't think Jake will eat those."

My heart soared: "next time"!!!

Then Matt took away his hand and sat back, and we watched the movie, which was so good (and Liam Carey was soooo handsome!) that I actually forgot about Matt for ninety minutes, and that's saying something!

After the movie, all the girls jumped up and ran to the ladies' room. There was lots to discuss.

"Okay, start from the beginning!" commanded Mia.

"Didn't you hear what happened? You were only a seat away," I said.

"We were busy watching the trailers," Katie said. "Now spill!"

I explained everything, and Emma moaned and put her hands on her head. "This is what I am always telling you guys! Jake is a menace! He ruins everything!"

"Awww, come on. He's so cute! How can you even stay mad at him?" Mia defended him.

"He's not cute," insisted Emma.

"I think he's a cute menace," I said with a grin.

"So does this mean you'll come to the skating party tomorrow?" asked Katie.

"I'll definitely come," I agreed. "I have to help bring the cupcakes, anyway. I don't think I'll skate, though." Now that I was fired up about Matt again, I *really* didn't want him to see me wobbling around on ice skates, Sasha or no Sasha.

"That's so lame! You have to skate. You took that lesson!" said Katie.

"I know, but I'll look like such a fool in front of Matt. You can't believe how bad I am."

"You'll just have to skate with us," said Katie. "We're your friends, and we don't care how you look on the ice. It will be fun. And we can hide you from Matt if you need us to. That's all there is to it."

"Maybe," I said, knowing there was no way I'd do it now. "Come on, we'd better get out there, or those guys might leave."

"Trust me, they are not leaving," Mia said with a laugh. But, still, we all took one last look in the mirror (I still hardly recognized myself), and we turned to leave.

But Emma caught me by the arm and whispered so the others couldn't hear. "I knew he liked you! Don't you ever worry about it again, and don't ever change. He likes you just the way you are— straight hair or curly, fancy clothes or plain, good skater or spaz. He likes you, and *I love you!*" She gave me a tight sideways squeeze.

"Thanks, Em. Love ya, too."

"I knew I'd seen that little candy basket and ribbon somewhere before," she muttered, shaking her head. "Oh, Jake. That little rat!"

Outside, the boys were playing arcade games, and we stood around and watched for a little while. It was almost six o'clock, and I'd have to get home soon, but George suggested we all walk across the mall for some pizza. We checked with our parents, and they extended our pick-up time to six thirty, so we raced to the pizzeria.

I caught up to Jake as we speed walked and said, "Hey, Jake, uh, do you think you'd let me have that ribbon for my memory box? I'll give you another one just like it." I knew Mia would let me have hers. I knew it was silly, but I just wanted some part of the very first gift I'd ever received from a boy, even though I didn't actually receive the gift.

"Sure," agreed Jake, stopping dead in the middle of the mall. He unzipped his backpack, carefully undid the ribbon, and handed it to me with a serious look on his face. "I'm sorry, Alexis. I shouldn't have taken your things."

"That's okay, bud. I forgive you. And I know how hard it is to resist a Cupcake Club masterpiece." I tousled his hair and he grinned.

The boys came up behind us then, and I shoved the ribbon into my pocket before Matt could see what we were doing.

"Alexis wanted your ribbon," said Jake, and I turned beet red.

Oh, Jake! I thought. *Right after I defended you!*

"Oh yeah?" said Matt. "And I wanted her cupcake!" he added, without missing a beat.

Now Jake blushed. "Sorry, Matty."

"Aw, that's all right. I'll just have to shake it out of you!" And he whipped Jake off his feet, turned him upside down and began shaking him by the ankles, while Jake laughed hysterically and I admired Matt's strength.

"Come on!" George called. "Stop showing off for Alexis and let's get this pizza, or it will be too late!"

Matt put down Jake, and we three walked toward the food court. Panda Gardens was closed.

"Ooh, sorry," I said to Matt. "We'll miss you, Panda Gardens!" I called, cupping my hands on either side of my mouth.

He laughed and pulled my hands away.

"Nice try. They don't serve dinner on Thursdays. Night off."

"Oh! Phew!" I said. "That's good news." I really didn't want Panda Gardens to close because I know how much Matt loves their food.

"Hey, Valentine's Day is kind of a silly holiday,

isn't it?" Matt asked as we arrived at Pinocchio's Pizza.

I hesitated. I wasn't sure how to say what I felt. But then I took a deep breath. "I think it sometimes causes more harm than good, unless you sell greeting cards and candy."

Matt laughed. "That's true," he said.

My mom would have been proud.

CHAPTER 12

Cupcake Panda-monium

*P*anda cupcakes aren't as easy to make as they look.

For one thing, M&M's for ears are heavy, and they don't want to stay put when you wedge them into the outer edge of soft frosting, which is where they show them in the pictures online.

For another thing, it takes a skilled hand and lots of time and patience to make little brown-featured faces over and over again.

We learned this the hard way, at Katie's house on Friday.

The four of us Cupcakers had gone to Katie's straight from school, and we'd planned to decorate the cupcakes, then head to our respective homes to shower, change, and primp (except Mia, who'd brought her stuff, so she could get ready at Katie's).

Then we agreed we'd regroup at Katie's to bring the cupcakes to the skating party together.

Only with the cupcakes taking so long, we ran out of time to go home. And to shower. And to change.

Did I mention that making panda cupcakes is also messy work?

Here's what happened: We frosted the chocolate cupcakes in white frosting, then we let that set for a little while. We were thinking we'd just whip through the faces, so . . . maybe we watched *Ballroom Dancing* for a little too long. But we were also tired, it had been a long week—the usual. So we had about an hour left to do the decorating, then an hour to go home and change.

Mia and Katie started on the decorating, with me and Emma kind of watching, since they're the two who are good at "pretty." (Though I am a wiz at fondant flowers; it's my specialty.)

Mia cut the end off a tube of brown gel frosting and put the M&M's in a bowl. Then she looked at the photo I'd printed from the Internet and began to do the first face.

"Wow, this is kind of . . . hard," she admitted. "You have to stop after each feature and get the frosting to stop coming out before you can move on to the next. See? Each cupcake is going to take a long time."

"What?" I asked, peering over her shoulder. I knew they had this covered, so I wasn't that engaged.

"Watch." Mia piped a blob for one eye, then she reached for a knife on the table and nicked the drip of frosting, so it wouldn't drag across the bear's white face. Then she did a blob for the next eye, then she had to do the same thing with the knife again to stop the frosting. Then she piped a nose. ("It's impossible to make this a triangle. Sorry, Lex," she said with a shrug. "I can't imagine how they got it to look like that in the photo.") Then she nicked the drip and then piped the mouth with a line connecting it to the nose.

"Wow. Slow," she said, blowing upward with her mouth to get a stray strand of hair off her face.

"Who's doing the ears?" she asked.

Katie offered, and she took the cupcake and stuck the ears into the top edge of the cupcake frosting, right above the eyes.

Emma tipped her head and looked. "Cute. Ish. It will get better as you do more, Katie, I'm sure. That's just the first one."

And then—*plink, plink!* The M&M's fell out of the frosting and onto the table.

122

"Wait, why's that happening?" I asked.

"The frosting's not stiff enough, darn it!" said Katie. She reached for two new M&M's (the previous ones were covered in white frosting and wouldn't work). "What if we put them in a little deeper, like this?" she asked, wedging the M&M's more on top of the frosting, kind of above the panda's eyes.

"Well, they're supposed to be coming off the top of its head. That's what makes it look like a panda," I said. "How long will it take for the frosting to stiffen?" I asked.

"Longer than we have," Mia said with a grimace as she looked at the clock.

Emma was biting her lip. "Also, I hate to say it, but if we have the ears coming off the head and we try to put them in the cupcake carriers, they might not fit. They'll just get knocked off as we put each cake into its slot."

I put my head in my hands and moaned. "Is this just a total fail? Now we have three-day-old cupcakes that look bad, too."

"They'll be fine. Kids don't care, anyway," Katie said, bustling over to help Mia. "But I think it's all hands on deck now. Just put the ears where they'll stay." She handed us each a tube of brown frosting, and the kitchen fell silent as we all got to work. Soon we each had a knife in one hand as we got better at wielding the gel tubes. The M&M's ears looked funny, but it was too late to do anything else.

"These don't really scream panda," Emma said at one point.

"Panda!" I screamed, and everyone laughed.

"Well, it *was* a good idea," Katie said kindly. "Thanks, Alexis. Very creative."

"Don't worry, my feelings aren't hurt. It's fine," I said. "I just wish we had done a test batch first, the way we usually do. But these looked like they'd be easy from the photos! Oh well. Live and learn."

I'd set a pretty high bar at the movies yesterday, appearance wise, and I knew I'd have to look great again tonight. Dylan had laid out another outfit for me and had promised to help with hair and makeup. (I'd taken perfect care of her sweater, leaving it neatly folded, with tissue, on her bed, and a five-dollar iTunes gift card I'd gotten for my birthday, sitting on top as a thank-you gift, so she was waaaay into me right now.)

At some point, Mrs. Brown came home from work, and she began helping, too. Because she's a dentist, she has a steady hand, so she can pipe frosting like a pro. I kept looking at the clock as we went into our final hour, and with not a lot of time left until we had to leave, and with flecks of white frosting, as well as blobs of brown, all over my blue T-shirt and jeans, I started to panic.

"I . . . Would you guys mind if I called home to see if someone could bring my outfit over here?" I asked. There goes Dylan's professional hair and makeup; now Matt will probably think I look awful, I thought sadly.

"Great idea!" agreed Emma.

I dialed home and was lucky enough to get my mom on the phone, and she agreed to bring the outfit on my bed, plus swing by Emma's to pick up her outfit. So Emma called her mom to tell her what to put out, and then we went back to the decorating. It was just. So. Slow.

My mom arrived about fifteen minutes later and stayed to chat with Mrs. Brown. After a few minutes, she realized we were totally in the weeds, so she sat down and got to work too.

And then disaster struck.

With about two dozen cupcakes left to go, we ran out of brown frosting!

We had to leave for the party in fifteen minutes.

My mom and Mrs. Brown told us to run upstairs and change, and they'd figure it out. So we raced up to Katie's room and put on our outfits. There was no time for showers, so we took turns washing our faces in the bathroom and brushing out hair. Katie generously offered us makeup and perfume and anything we wanted, but I'm not so good at putting that stuff on, and I was so stressed about the cupcakes, I just wanted to get dressed and get downstairs.

I threw on the cute outfit, which wasn't too dressy (certainly not like yesterday's)—dark-washed jeans; a pink long-sleeved T-shirt; a raspberry-colored, fitted fleece vest; and a batik scarf in pinks that I'd wound around my neck a few times, like Dylan showed me. To finish it off, my new pink ski hat. Dylan had also lent me these elaborate lace-up brown leather boots that were really complicated to put on and take off. Since I wouldn't be skating, I hadn't minded when she'd shown me how long it would take to put them on. But now that we were running so late, I didn't have time to fuss with them. I jammed my feet back into my plain brown clogs and clomped back downstairs to see if the moms had come up with a solution. And they had!

Mrs. Brown was at the stove, stirring something in a pot. I sniffed the air.

"Yum! Chocolate sauce?" I asked.

"I had an idea!" said my mom. She looked down into the pot. "That looks about right. And we don't want it too hot."

Mrs. Brown poured the sauce into a little bowl and handed my mom a tiny clean paintbrush.

"I'm going to practice first," said my mom. "It's been a while!"

"What are you doing?" I asked, intrigued.

My mom took a thickly folded paper towel, dipped the paintbrush into the chocolate sauce, and then painted a quick series of graceful interconnected lines on the paper towel.

"Pretty!" said Mrs. Brown.

My mom stood back and assessed it. "Huh. Looks pretty good! Now I'll try it on a cupcake."

"It looks like Chinese writing," I said, coming around the table to look more closely.

"It is," my mom said quietly. "It's the Chinese character for 'love.' The word is *ai*."

"Cool!" cried Mia, who had arrived back in the kitchen. Katie and Emma arrived too, and we explained it to them.

"That's perfect!" said Emma. "Because it was Valentine's Day, and now it's Chinese New Year, and so it's love and Chinese and . . . How do you know how to do that, Mrs. Becker?"

Duh! I hadn't thought to ask that myself. "Yeah, Mom. How *do* you know how to do that?"

My mom's cheeks turned a little pink, and she laughed. "Oh, well. I learned it a long time ago."

"Did you study Chinese?" asked Emma.

My mom glanced nervously at me, then she sighed. "The truth is, I had a huge crush in college on a boy who was Chinese. I wanted to make him a card, like a love note, so I learned how to write the character for love in Chinese calligraphy from a friend of mine."

"That's so romantic!" Mia sighed.

"Did it work?" asked Katie.

My mom shook her head. "Sadly, no. My crush was one-sided."

"I'm sorry, Mom. That's sad," I said.

"Well, everything turned out for the best, and I met your dad after all, and he was just right for me! I just wish I hadn't wasted so much time and energy on that boy." She dipped her brush in the sauce and painted a perfect Chinese symbol on a cupcake. It looked great.

"Well, I, for one, am glad you did, or we wouldn't be able to salvage the rest of these cupcakes!" Mia laughed.

"Yeah!" we all agreed.

But I was watching my mom closely, and she turned and gave me a small smile and a wink. I nodded. I now knew why she was so concerned about me and the time I was spending thinking about Matt. She wanted to protect me, maybe from heartbreak. Besides wanting me to be independent and everything, of course.

I went over and hugged her before she dipped her brush again. "Thanks, Mom," I whispered. "I *ai* you."

"*Wo ai ni,*" she said. "That's how you say it in Chinese."

"*Wo ai ni*, then."

We made it to the skating party only ten minutes late, and who was the first person I ran into but Sasha! After we settled the cupcakes on the buffet and the PTA president paid me, I introduced Sasha to all the Cupcakers, and we chatted for a while before she left for the night.

"Wait until you see Alexis skate tonight!" Sasha said proudly. "She is my star student! Such a fast learner!"

"Oh, well ... I'm not so sure I will skate tonight," I said, shrugging. "You know. I'm not ready for prime-time viewing!"

"Don't be silly! You must practice to be good! Now is opportunity, and you can show your friends too!"

I felt bad. Sasha had worked hard with me and was pleased with what she'd accomplished, and I was kind of blowing it off.

"Well, maybe I'll just rent the skates, and then we'll see . . . ," I said.

"Get skates, come back, and I tie them properly for you. Go now. I wait," she ordered.

"Okay, okay," I agreed. I went to stand on the rental line, which was unfortunately very short. I got my skates too fast and was back in a jiffy.

"Sit, sit," said Sasha. My friends sat too, to put their skates on, and then we were all ready. "Come!" commanded Sasha. She led the way down the ramp. She was even tinier without her skates on.

"Is Matt here already?" I whispered to Emma, frantically scanning the crowd on the ice for any sign of him.

"I'm not sure. I think he had practice, so he was coming late."

"Phew." I gave a huge sigh of relief. "So maybe I can get this over with before he gets here."

"You mean you can warm up, so you're ready

when he arrives!" said Sasha, who'd been eaves-
dropping.

"Busted!" cried Mia, and we all laughed. We'd
reached the door to the ice. Ugh.

"Now go, my little prodigy. Skate and have fun!"
Sasha said with a smile.

"Hi, Sasha!" cried someone. Ugh. Olivia Allen,
of course—right as I'm about to get on the ice.

I froze. I didn't want to do this.

"You did a great job teaching Alexis to skate the
other night," continued Olivia. "It took me months
to learn what she did in one night. It was impressive." Olivia pushed by us and went out on the ice.
I glanced at Sasha, and I could tell she was pleased.
I was glad Olivia had been nice to Sasha and hoped
it had something to do with what I'd said.

"Well," said Sasha, embarrassed.

"Thanks, Sasha!" I said. Then I walked onto the
ice and fell down.

Just kidding!

I stepped gracefully over the threshold, and
holding onto the side, I began to skate.

"Push, then glide!" called Sasha from behind
me. I knew if I turned, I would fall, so I just waved
and kept skating.

Suddenly, someone whooshed up next to me.

I hoped it wasn't Olivia! I turned just the tiniest amount.

Matt.

"Hi!" he said with a grin.

I grinned back. "I heard you were at practice," I said.

"Canceled because of the party," he said. "They knew no one would come." He shrugged. "Want to skate?"

"Oh. I'm sure you're much better than I am, so why don't you just go ahead, and I'll catch— Whoa!" Matt had grabbed my hands like Sasha had and begun skating, strong but not too fast, around the rink. He took me on a loop, and as I passed the entrance, I saw Sasha grinning widely and waving. I wasn't about to let go of his hands, so I just grinned back like an idiot.

The best thing about being a bad skater is having someone hold your hands when they skate with you. Especially someone cute, who you are totally crushing on.

"It's so embarrassing being a bad skater," I said.

"Well, no one has to be to be great at everything. And you're great at so many other things," said Matt. "Feeling embarrassed is really a waste of time."

Then Matt leaned in next to me. "By the way, you looked really pretty with your hair and everything yesterday, but I just wanted you to know you look pretty just all normal like this. Prettier."

I laughed and blushed. "Thanks. I guess I'm just a normal kind of girl."

"Alexis Becker, you are way, way above normal," said Matt. "And don't you ever let anyone tell you otherwise."

And we skated around and around. *Ah, Mom would love him, too. Wo ai ni*—I thought (but would never say!)—*Wo ai ni.*

Want another sweet cupcake?
Here's a sneak peek
of the next book in the

CUPCAKE ◆ DIARIES

series:

Katie
sprinkled
secrets

Good Secrets, Bad Secrets

Sometimes I can't believe how much I've changed since I've started middle school. On the first day of school, my best friend, Callie Wilson, dumped me because she didn't think I was as popular as her new friends. But now I have three best friends: Mia Velaz-Cruz, Alexis Becker, and Emma Taylor, and they are really great.

I used to think boys were just, well, boys. But now I have a sort-of boyfriend named George Martinez.

I used to think it would be really bad if my mom ever got a boyfriend. But now she's dating Jeff—who I have to call Mr. Green sometimes, because he's a teacher at my school—and it's not bad at all.

I used to bake in my spare time. But now

I bake almost all the time, because my friends and I have a real business selling cupcakes—the Cupcake Club.

I also used to be really against the idea of joining a competitive sports team at school. I would just get too nervous about the whole thing, and then I would make all these goofy mistakes. But now, well, things are different.

"Katie, I don't get it," Emma said during lunch in the cafeteria one day. "Why did you join the track team? I mean, it's great, but I thought you just liked to run for fun."

"Well, I was really anxious about it," I admitted. "But Jeff—I mean, Mr. Green—is friends with Coach Goodman, the track coach. And the track team is the one team you don't try out for—anyone can join. So even if I don't run in any races, it might be fun to run with a group of people."

"And Coach Goodman is so nice!" Mia added. "I have her for Technology. She makes everything seem so easy."

I nodded. "Yeah, she's supernice. She took me aside in the hall and said she heard I was a good runner. She said I could come to a practice and check it out. She doesn't put a lot of pressure on the team, but everybody tries really hard, anyway, you know? So it seemed good, and I just thought I should go for it."

"That's really great," said Alexis. Her curly red hair bounced on her shoulders as she nodded. "You know, any activities you do will look great on your college application. It's never too early to start." We all rolled our eyes but laughed because Alexis is always thinking about things like that.

"I think you'll be great," Emma added, smiling. "You're an awesome runner!"

"Thanks," I said. "I don't know how I'll do in a real race, though. Coach Goodman says I should do the long-distance races, the 800-meter or the 1,600-meter. And maybe a relay."

"E-mail me your practice and meet schedule when you get it," Alexis said. "It's getting harder and harder to schedule our Cupcake Club meetings these days."

Each of us in the Cupcake Club brings something different to the team. Alexis is a business whiz and keeps us really organized. Mia is a great artist, and she comes up with amazing cupcake decorations. Emma and I are really good at coming up with new recipes and flavors. (I'm not sure about Emma, but I know that I dream about cupcakes sometimes—honestly. Once I dreamed that these mini marshmallows were dancing around a swimming pool filled with caramel, and then they all jumped in. That's how my famous marshmallow-caramel cupcake was born.)

"Are we still meeting Friday night?" Mia asked.

Alexis scrolled down her phone screen. "Yes. Seven o'clock at my house."

"Can we do it at eight?" Emma asked. "I have a modeling job after school, and it might go a little late."

"Anything exciting?" Mia asked, her dark eyes shining. Mia's mom is a fashion stylist, and Mia wants to design clothes someday. Which is fine with me because she wants to go to design school in Manhattan, and I want to go to cooking school in Manhattan. This way we won't have to say good-bye forever after high school—not that we would, anyway, but I'm glad we're planning to stay close.

Emma frowned. "It's a summer preview catalog, so it's lots of shorts and tank tops," she said. "Which means I have to shave my legs."

Emma was wearing a skirt, and I ducked and looked at her legs. "Seriously? Your hair is so blond you can't even see it."

"The camera sees everything," Emma said in a serious tone. "Plus, they told me to." She sighed.

"Dylan says once you start shaving your leg hair, it grows in even more," Alexis said. (Dylan is her older sister, who's in high school.) "And I think she's right. I woke up the other morning, and I swear my leg hairs grew an inch."

The conversation was making me kind of uncomfortable. I had never even thought about shaving my legs. Honestly, I never even noticed that everyone else started doing it.

"I hate doing it," said Mia. "Don't you, Katie?"

Mia is my closest friend. If we were alone, maybe I would have told the truth right then. Instead, I lied.

"Yeah, it's the worst," I agreed, even though I had no idea what it was like. Then I quickly changed the subject. "So, yeah, eight o'clock on Friday is fine with me for a meeting."

"Me too," Mia said.

"Then eight o'clock it is," Alexis said, typing into her phone. She put it down and opened up her lunch container. "Mmm, Asian chicken salad. Gotta make a note to thank Dad."

"Yeah, he's getting pretty creative with your lunches," I said.

"Once I pointed out that packing lunch was cheaper than buying lunch in the cafeteria every day, he gave in," she said. "I give him a shopping list to make things easier."

Emma poked at the spaghetti on her plate. "Well, I kind of like the cafeteria food. But now I have nobody to wait with on the lunch line."

"Sorry, Emma. I didn't think of that," Alexis said.

"I'd eat the school lunch, but I think packing lunch for me is one of Mom's hobbies," I said. I opened up my new bento box, which is a kind of Japanese lunch box. There are little compartments and containers, so you can have lots of different tastes in one meal.

"See? Carrot sticks and ranch dip, and she made me homemade cucumber sushi, and a hard-boiled egg, and grapes with a sweet dipping sauce."

"That is impressive," Mia said. "I've got a turkey and Swiss on a spinach wrap. Not superexciting, but it's my favorite, so . . ." She shrugged and took a bite. Then her cell phone made a chirping noise.

Mia picked it up and looked at the screen. Her eyes went wide.

"No way!" she said, shaking her head.

"Who's it from?" I asked.

"Olivia Allen," she replied. "She says that Julie Fletcher was seen at the mall with Todd Weiser."

"So?" I asked.

"*So?*" Mia said loudly. "Everybody knows that Todd is seeing Bella Kovacs!"

"Why would Olivia be texting that?" asked Emma. "Isn't Bella supposed to be her friend?"

Olivia and Bella are in a club together—the Best Friends Club. Callie (my former best friend) and Maggie Rodriguez are in it too. You have to be really popular to be in the BFC. I think you have to be a little mean, too, but some of them are nicer than others. Mia could be in the club if she wanted to, but she'd rather stick with us. (Which is another reason why I love her.)

"Well, Olivia is not exactly what you'd call great friend material," Mia pointed out, and we all nodded. When she first came to Park Street Middle School, Mia had been really nice to her. But Olivia didn't appreciate it one bit, and she ended up doing some really mean things to Mia. So Mia ended their friendship. Olivia has been a little nicer lately. But she'll never be one of the Cupcakers.

"You can say that again," I said. "She's not great at keeping a secret, either."

Mia laughed. "You're right, Katie, but since when are you good at keeping secrets?"

I was shocked. "What do you mean?"

"I know what she means," said Alexis, looking at me. "Like that time Emma, you, and I chipped in to get Mia that cool professional sketching kit for her birthday, and we wanted to keep it a surprise, but you blurted it out a week before the party."

I blushed. That had definitely happened. "Okay, well, that was because I was superexcited and couldn't control myself," I admitted. "But I didn't do it to hurt anybody's feelings. Olivia might have seen Julie and Todd at the mall, but she didn't have to say anything. Or she could have told Bella privately, instead of texting everybody."

Emma nodded. "Katie's right. Sometimes when you tell a secret, it can really hurt somebody."

"But sometimes you have to tell a secret, if it means it will keep somebody from being hurt," Mia pointed out.

"Well, I hate secrets," Alexis announced. "I mean, birthday surprises and stuff are okay, I guess. But I think if everybody was honest with one another all the time, it would save a lot of hurt feelings and trouble, you know?"

"Exactly," I said. "Some secrets are good, and some secrets are bad."

I looked over at the BFC table. Olivia and Bella

were sitting next to each other, and Bella was laughing about something. She had no idea that Olivia was spreading rumors that might hurt her.

Mia saw me looking at Bella.

"Yeah, I guess that text was a pretty bad one," she said. "Gossip can be really fun, but I guess it mostly stinks, you know?"

"Definitely," I agreed. "You know, I'm really glad we all don't keep secrets from one another." Then I briefly thought of the lie I had told about shaving my legs just minutes before—but that didn't count, did it? It was just a little white lie.

"Me too," my friends agreed, pretty much at the same time.

We finished our lunch and didn't talk about secrets anymore. That's because none of us knew it yet, but secrets were about to nearly tear apart the Cupcake Club.

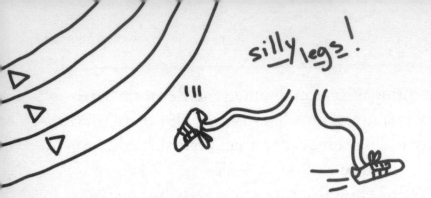

silly legs!

Did She Really Say That?

$\mathcal{M}$y first track practice was the next day, right after school. I was worried about things like whether I would be good enough or fast enough for the team. I wasn't thinking about secrets at all that first day— but as it turns out, maybe I should have.

Both the boys' and girls' teams practiced at the middle school field. There's a track that goes around the field for the running events, and the events like the shot put and long jump take place on the field part. Coach Goodman had told me to go to the girls' locker room to change before practice each day.

When I got to the locker room, I scanned to see who else I knew who was on the team. There was Hana Hancock, from my drama class. She was one of the tallest girls in our grade, and I figured that would make her a pretty good runner. I'm not supershort or supertall, just average, but I know I could probably run faster with long legs like Hana's.

Then I saw Natalie Egan, who's in my Spanish class. She's almost as tall as Hana, and I started to get nervous. Was I too short for the track team? Was there even such a thing as being too short for the track team? What if I lost every single race? What if I started too early, or tripped? My mind started racing.

You're just being silly, Katie, I told myself. *There are plenty of girls in the locker room who are shorter than you are. Stop worrying!*

While I was having this conversation with myself, I heard a voice behind me.

"Hi, Katie!"

I spun around to see a girl with blue eyes and long blond hair in a ponytail. It was Callie, my former best friend.

"So, I heard you were joining the team," she said. "I guess it's true."

"Yeah, Coach Goodman convinced me," I replied. "She's really nice."

Callie nodded. "Yeah, she is. Well, glad you're on

the team." Then she walked away to talk to some other girls.

That's how things are with Callie and me these days. Friendly, but nothing more. Our days of being besties are over. For a while, I was pretty mad at her, and she was not so nice to me. But we got over that stuff and made a kind of truce. I was actually glad she was on the team too. We're almost exactly the same height, so I didn't feel so short anymore.

I quickly changed into blue shorts, running shoes, and my official blue Park Street Middle School track team T-shirt. It felt pretty good to put it on, but scary at the same time. I took a deep breath and followed the other girls outside.

It was a chilly spring afternoon, and I shivered a little. But I knew that soon enough I would be starting to sweat. Coach Goodman walked up to us, wearing a blue tracksuit. She has red curly hair that reminds me of Alexis. Today, she kept it pulled back with a light blue bandana.

"Hello, girls' track team!" she said with a friendly smile. "Let's give a big cheer for our first practice of the year!"

We all clapped and yelled, "Wooooo!" Then Coach Goodman clapped her hands together. We settled down and paid attention.

"Okay, so for these first few practices we're going to work on form," she said. "Before we start drills, let's warm up and go for a jog."

She led us to a small grassy area near the main field to start stretches, and then we headed onto the track.

"This is not a race!" Coach Goodman called out as she led us around the track. "We just want to get your heart pumping."

It was one of those days when it just felt good to be outside. There were fluffy white clouds in the sky, and the silver bleachers on the side of the track looked shiny and clean and ready for the season. Somehow, I ended up jogging right between Hana and Natalie. I guess we were all keeping the same pace.

"Hey, Katie!" Natalie said, giving me a friendly smile.

"You know Katie?" asked Hana. "I know her too."

"Awesome," said Natalie.

"So, were you guys both on the team before?" I asked.

Hana nodded. "Since we started middle school."

"Coach Goodman seems nice," I said.

"She is," Natalie agreed. "She makes us work

hard, but she's not mean about it."

When the jog ended, I was feeling pretty good, and I wasn't out of breath or anything. I run with my mom all the time. We run together a lot of weekends. We'll just throw on our gear and head over to our local park. We've even done races and stuff.

Then Coach Goodman had us line up on the track using the lanes. I stuck to Hana and Natalie and got behind them.

"Form drills might seem weird or boring, but we do them for a reason," said Coach Goodman. "They'll help develop certain muscle groups to give you a better stride, make you a better runner, and prevent you from getting injured."

I started to get a little nervous. I thought running was just . . . running. What was all this about form and muscle groups?

"We'll start out with some high knees," said Coach Goodman. "For now, keep your hands still on your sides. Stand up straight. Now, lift up one knee at a time. Kind of like you're marching in place. Left . . . right . . . left."

We all started doing what Coach Goodman instructed.

"Slow now. That's it. Keep your thigh parallel to

the ground," Coach Goodman said.

I looked down at my legs. Parallel? That meant I should keep my thighs straight, like a table. I adjusted my movements a little.

"Okay, now add arm movements," said Coach Goodman, bending her arms at the elbow and pumping them back and forth.

Once we had done that for a while, she told us to go faster.

"Just pick up the pace," she said. "There we go! Keep those knees high."

We did it faster, and I started giggling. I couldn't help it. We all looked pretty silly!

"Glad you're having fun, Katie," Coach Goodman called out, but she was smiling, not being sarcastic or scolding, thank goodness. I smiled back.

Once we got used to the faster pace, Coach told us to start walking while we did high knees. We high-kneed our way around the track.

"We look like prancing ponies," I said, giggling again. Hana and Natalie started giggling too.

"You'll get used to it," Hana promised.

After we completed a lap around the track, we lined up at the starting line. I didn't feel too winded, but I could feel a slight burning in my legs. I guess I was developing those muscle groups!

I thought high knees was a pretty silly exercise, but then it got even worse.

"Okay," Coach Goodman said. "Time for butt kicks!"

"Is that what I think it is?" I asked.

"Yup," Natalie said with a nod.

For the butt kicks, we had to keep our backs straight, facing forward, and kick back our heels so that they almost touched our butts.

Now, I can tell everyone that track practice kicked my butt! I thought, and then I burst out giggling. Coach looked over at me and raised an eyebrow, and I turned my attention back to kicking my butt.

When we finished the butt kicks, things got even weirder! We did this thing called high skips, where we had to basically skip as we ran while swinging arms.

"This is great training that will help you push off at the start of a race," Coach Goodman explained as we collapsed into giggles after having finished a lap of high skips. I mean, we looked pretty ridiculous! But even though it was weird, I realized I was having fun.

We did the drills all over again—high knees, butt kicks, and high skips. As we were skipping around the field again, the boys started to come onto the field. Their practice started right after ours.

I was high-skipping down the track when George, my sort-of boyfriend, walked up to the fence in his blue track uniform. He's on the boys' team, and that was one more reason I joined the girls' team. He told me how much fun it was. Plus, he pointed out that we could spend time with each other at the meets. It made me really happy when he'd told me that.

"Hey, look! It's Silly Legs!" he called out.

I wasn't expecting him to call me out like that, and I tripped over my own feet, catching myself before I could fall down. Then I stuck out my tongue at him and kept going.

I wasn't offended by what he said. George and I have known each other since elementary school. I'm a terrible volleyball player, and he used to tease me by calling me "Silly Arms" in gym class whenever we played. Once I realized he wasn't trying to be mean, the nickname didn't bother me.

But having him yell out "Silly Legs" like that—especially on my first day of track practice—threw me off a little bit. I kept skipping, but I knew I wasn't doing it perfectly. I also knew George was watching me, and I started to feel kind of self-conscious.

Katie's New Recipe 13

Mia a Matter of Taste 14

Emma Sugar and Spice and Everything Nice 15

Alexis and the Missing Ingredient 16

Katie Sprinkles & Surprises 17

Mia Fashion Plates and Cupcakes 18

Emma: Lights! Camera! Cupcakes! 19

Alexis the Icing on the Cupcake 20

Katie Starting from Scratch 21

Mia's Recipe for Disaster 22

Emma's Not-So-Sweet Dilemma 23

Alexis's Cupcake Cupid 24

Katie Sprinkled Secrets 25

Want more

CUPCAKE 🧁 DIARIES?

Visit **CupcakeDiariesBooks.com**
for the series trailer, excerpts, activities,
and everything you need for throwing
your own cupcake party!

Coco Simon always dreamed of opening a cupcake bakery but was afraid she would eat all of the profits. When she's not daydreaming about cupcakes, Coco edits children's books and has written close to one hundred books for children, tweens, and young adults, which is a lot less than the number of cupcakes she's eaten. Cupcake Diaries is the first time Coco has mixed her love of cupcakes with writing.